THE MADNESS OF WAITING

THE MADNESS OF WAITING
MUHAMMAD HADI RUSWĀ

A Translation of
JUNŪN-E INTEZĀR YA'NĪ FASĀNĀ-E MIRZĀ RUSWĀ
by MIRZĀ MUHAMMAD HADI RUSWĀ

Krupa Shandilya
Taimoor Shahid

zubaan

ZUBAAN

an imprint of Kali for Women

128 B Shahpur Jat, 1st floor
New Delhi 110 049
EMAIL contact@zubaanbooks.com
WEBSITE www.zubaanbooks.com

First published by Zubaan 2012

10 9 8 7 6 5 4 3 2 1

ISBN   978 93 81017708

Zubaan is an independent feminist publishing house
based in New Delhi with a strong academic and general
list. It was set up as an imprint of India's first feminist
publishing house, Kali for Women, and carries forward
Kali's tradition of publishing world quality books to high
editorial and production standards. *Zubaan* means tongue,
voice, language, speech in Hindustani. Zubaan is a non-
profit publisher, working in the areas of the humanities,
social sciences, as well as in fiction, general non-fiction,
and books for children and young adults under its Young
Zubaan imprint.

Designed by Sunandini Banerjee, Seagull Books
Printed at Raj Press, R-3 Inderpuri, New Delhi 110 012

CONTENTS

AN INTRODUCTION

Umrāo Jān's Story:
Urdu Literary Culture and the Courtesan
in Late-nineteenth Century India

This translation is the product of a transnational collaboration that came about quite by accident. Growing up in Mumbai, India, I was very well-versed with the character of Umrāo Jān through her countless iterations in films and television serials. I had of course read the novel *Umrāo Jān Adā* by M.H. Ruswā on which these adaptations were based. As a student of literature, the enduring popularity of *Umrāo Jān Adā*, both the novel and the character, intrigued me. In June 2007 I began researching the novel with the hope of writing a chapter comparing Umrāo Jān's depiction in the novel with popular representations of her for my doctoral thesis.

In the course of my research I discovered C.M. Naim's translation of the first extant review of *Umrāo Jān Adā*, which suggested the existence of a sequel to *Umrāo Jān Adā— Jūnūn-e Intezār Yā'nī Fasāna'-e Mirzā Ruswā* (*The Madness of Waiting: The Story of Mirzā Ruswā*. The review is included in the appendix of this book). I emailed Dr Naim and asked him if he had come across this text. He said that he had no knowledge of any survi-ving copies. I spent the next month emailing librarians specialising in South Asia and writing to Urdu scholars asking them if they knew of the existence of this book, but no one had heard of it or seen it in print.

I had almost abandoned hope of recovering the lost sequel when I came across a reference to it on Carnegie Mellon's Million Book Project.[1] A scanned copy of the book had been uploaded as part of the Digital Libraries of India project.[2] From the scanned copy I discovered that the original document was housed at the Sālār Jang Museum in

1 The Million Book Project works with government and research partners in India and China to scan books in many languages and provides free access to the books on the web. As of 2007, they have completed the scanning of 1 million books and have made accessible the entire database from http://www.ulib.org

2 The Digital Libraries of India project partners with libraries across India to scan books and make them available for free through the Million Books Project.

Hyderabad, India. A travel grant from Cornell University enabled me to visit the Museum. It was after many hours of labouring in the archives and sifting through tattered leather-bound catalogues and registers that I managed to unearth the original. Unfortunately, the book had lost its original cover and was bound with frayed cardboard.

As I began to work on the translation, I became aware that literary resources essential to contextualising Ruswā, like the people of the subcontinent, had been divided arbitrarily across Pakistan and India. After being denied a visa to Pakistan, I became aware of the urgency of finding a partner who had access to resources in Pakistan and possessed a stronger grasp of Persianate Urdu. At the time I was studying Urdu with Bilal Shahid at Cornell University and he introduced me to his brother Taimoor in Pakistan who was also interested in Urdu literature. In one of our many phone conversations, I mentioned Ruswā's text and he was very excited to read it and help me with the translation. Even though we were separated by continents, thanks to the internet we were able to co-translate this text in a matter of a few months.

In what follows, we situate Ruswā within his literary and historical context. We analyse his fiction, literary style and views on literature in light of his contemporaries and in the context of the colonial discourse on Urdu literature. We then move on to examine Ruswā's complicated relationship with Umrāo Jān the courtesan, who appears in three of his novels: *Afshā-e Rāz, Umrāo Jān Adā* and *Jūnūn-e Intezār*. We study the evolution of her character across these novels and her relationship to her historical counterpart. We conclude by thinking of the implications of recovering Umrāo Jān's voice as 'narrator' and 'author' for the feminist archive.

Ruswā and Urdu Literary Culture at the Turn of the Nineteenth Century

Urdu literary culture reached its zenith in the mid-nineteenth century with the arrival of Ghālib, the great Urdu poet. At this historical moment, Urdu and Persian poetry enjoyed the royal patronage of the Mughal court and the admiration of the British colonial administration.[3] After the Revolt of 1857, Urdu

3 In *Nets of Awareness*, Frances Pritchett suggests that the Mughal court in Delhi was a centre for Urdu poetry before the Revolt: "Urdu poetry was widely and seriously cultivated: there were not only frequent mushairahs at

poetry and the Muslim elite became the targets of British criticism. At the trial of the last Mughal emperor, Bahādur Shāh, a key figure in the events of 1857, the English prosecutor argued that "to Mussulmān intrigue and Mahommedan conspiracy we may mainly attribute the dreadful calamities of the year 1857" (Pritchett 18). This launched the British programme of undermining Muslim life, culture and society. Specifically, the British criticised Urdu poetry as being depraved and licentious.[4]

In her book *Nets of Awareness,* Frances Pritchett attributes this critique to the imposition of Victorian categories of aesthetic judgment on Urdu poetry. As a result, at the turn of the nineteenth century, Urdu literary

the Red Fort, but also weekly ones held on the Delhi College premises,[19] as well as numerous privately sponsored ones. When it came to poets, Bahādur Shāh's circle included, besides himself, one great poet, several major ones, and literally dozens of highly competent minor poets" (Pritchett 6-7).

4 Pritchett suggests that Colonel Holroyd, the director of public instruction, was instrumental in the project of "reforming" Urdu poetry. In a public meeting of the *Anjuman-e Panjab*, Holyrod announced that "the official journal of the *Anjuman*" predicted full success in "removing from Urdu poetry licentious subjects and obscene images, and replacing them by scenes descriptive of things in this world" (Pritchett 36).

circles were divided between creating Urdu literature as an imitation of British literature and aesthetic sensibility and preserving the genres and aesthetics of Urdu literature. Pritchett suggests that critics Hāli and Āzād were of the view that poetry in every language undergoes cycles of birth, decay and destruction: the earliest poetry, in any literary tradition, is simple and 'natural' and best; when artifice creeps into its construction, it decays and rots.[5] This view of poetry was deeply influenced by English literary critics, who were celebrating the 'naturalness' of Romantic poetry. According to Hāli and Āzād, a turn to nature as a subject and to 'naturalness' as a style was necessary for the revitalization of Urdu poetry.

In contrast, Ruswā, a close friend of Hāli's, writes this about those who attempt to emulate the English:

5 "Hāli, like Āzād, saw this process as a universal problem: In every language natural poetry has always been the portion of the early poets (105). Later poets, by contrast, face grave risks. If they don't do anything but imitate, if they remain within the limits of this narrow circle of thoughts that the early poets have expressed, then their poetry gradually declines from a natural state—so much so that they end up very far from the straight road of nature(105-6)" (Pritchett 135).

A few poets of this country desire to bring the sensibilities of the English imagination to their pen, but this sensibility fails to arrive. On the other hand, there are those who wish to avoid it but it arrives. Time says: both these groups are foolish; their endeavors are pointless, and their efforts [will be] underappreciated. It is unreasonable to conclude that the Revolt wouldn't affect our literary sensibility. As one gentleman suggests, 'Slip into a new mould every day, when the times change, you too change with them.' Time replies, 'Arrived late but arrived eventually.' I, Ruswā, make others follow my course. (Fatehpuri 52)

From this it is evident that Ruswā sees those who emulate the English as losing sight of their own identity because they slip into any new "mould" available to them. However, at the same time he suggests that it is pointless to resist the influence of the English literary tradition. Ruswā's own fidelities are simultaneously to both the Urdu and English literary traditions. In the introduction to his first literary production, the *mathnavī Nau-Bahār* (*New Spring*) (1866), Ruswā writes: "I have suffused the English rose with the scent of jasmine."[6] One finds evidence of this in Ruswā's rewriting of George Reynolds' *Rosa Lambert* (1854-1855) in his novel *Umrāo Jān Adā*. The plot of Ruswā's novel is drawn from *Rosa Lambert*, but the setting of the novel and its cultural sensibility are indebted to Urdu literary culture.[7]

More specifically, the novel is situated a few years before the Revolt of 1857, the heyday of Urdu literary culture. As Fatehpuri demonstrates, Ruswā copied entire sections from *Qaisar al Tawārīkh* (*The Shah/ Sultan of Histories*), Kamaluddin Haider's historical treatise on the architecture and literary

6 *Mathnavī* is a form of verse in Arabic, Persian, Urdu, and Turkish. It is a long poem which usually narrates a story. It is written in internally rhyming couplets, which all have the same metre.

7 In this novel, Rosa Lambert, the young woman protagonist, is abducted from her father's house by villains and sold into prostitution. The subsequent events of the narrative delve into the moral dilemmas of its protagonist as Rosa attempts to preserve her 'honour' from being sullied at the hands of rogues, dandies and other immoral men but fails to do so. Most of the novel consists of Rosa's reflections on her sorry state, and thus the novel reinstates nineteenth century Victorian morality, even as it provides the reader with lascivious details of Rosa's transgressions.

culture of Awadh before 1857.[8] This era provides him with an idealized setting for his novel, which largely centres on the poetic and musical talents of his courtesan protagonist, Umrāo Jān Adā. Umrāo Jān's ability to shine in the era of literary greats such as Ghālib and Zauq suggests that she is exceptionally talented. She is a representation of the superior literary skills of *tawāifs* [courtesans] at this historical moment. Her depiction functions as a defiant rewriting of post-1857 English narratives that depict *tawāifs* as "nautch girls" who are part of a dissolute Lucknawi elite culture.[9] The novel is then uniquely situated simultaneously in the past and the present—its nostalgic portrayal of the

8 A telling example of this is as follows:

Qaisar al Tawārīkh

Mirzā Barjīs Qadar arrived . . . the Kashmīrīs sang the following *ghazal* for him:

> Birjīs Qadar is the honour of the moon/ Birjīs Qadar is a unique jewel (*Qaisar al Tawārīkh* 130)

Umrāo Jān Adā

The festival of Birjīs Qadar's eleventh birthday was celebrated with much pomp and splendour. In this gathering, the Kashmīrīs sang the following poem for him:

> Birjīs Qadar is the honour of the moon/ Birjīs Qadar is a unique jewel (*Umrāo Jān Adā* 184)

9 The "nautch girl" of the British imagination lacked "middle-class bourgeois 'respectability' " (Grewal 55), and was therefore seen as licentious and depraved.

superior literary culture of Lucknow society is used to defy contemporary and historical British perspectives of Urdu literary culture.

Curiously enough, despite Ruswā's adherence to Urdu literary culture, his novel does not seek to emulate the narrative form of the contemporary Urdu novel. At this historical moment, there were two dominant genres for the Urdu novel—the *dāstān* and the didactic novel. The term *dāstān* is used to refer specifically to folktales, fairytales and adventurous romances that include elements of the mythic and the fantastic. The *dāstān* in Urdu draws from a longer Persio-Arabic tradition. Historically, the *dāstān* was passed down from generation to generation through oral narration. As a particular *dāstān* circulated in different regions, its stories were embellished and local details were added to make it more exciting to its audience. With the advent of a vernacular printing press in South Asia, Persian *dāstāns* such as such as *Dāstān-e Amīr Hamzā*, *Alf Lailā*, *Bostān-e K hayāl*, were translated into Urdu, published, and

10 In 1871, Naval Kishore Press in Lucknow published a very popular version of *Dāstān-e Amīr Hamzā* that continued to be republished well into the twentieth century (Musharraf Ali Faruqi, *The Adventures of Amir Hamza*, xxviii, 2007).

widely circulated.[10] This paved the way for a spate of *dāstān*-inspired Urdu 'novels' such as *Fasāna'-e 'Ajāib* by Rajab Ali Surūr of Lucknow and *Fasāna'-e 'Azād* by Pandit Rathan Nāth Sarshār. Although not of the same literary quality as the *dāstāns* of the Persio-Arabic tradition, these Urdu *dāstāns* remained popular with readers. New *dāstāns* continued to be written until the early years of the twentieth century, when they finally gave way to the realist novel which was becoming increasingly popular.

In the middle and late nineteenth century, the Urdu novel was also mobilized as a form of celebrating a glorious Muslim past and reviving a Muslim identity in response to Sir Syed Ahmed Khan's call to reform Muslim society from within.[11] In his essay

11 The Aligarh movement (1858-1898) spearheaded by Sir Syed Ahmad Khan attempted to reform Muslim society by making it more like English society by introducing discipline, order and high levels of education. Sir Syed Ahmad's disdain for his countrymen's "native" indifference to their condition was heightened after a visit to Britain. He returned brimming with ideas for reforming Muslim society: "The natives of India . . . when contrasted with the English in education, manners and uprightness, are like them as a dirty animal is to an able and handsome man" (Sir Sayyid Ahmad Khan; quoted in Jones 65). Jones observes in his study of the Aligarh movement's reformist impetus: "To end this state of decadence Sayyid Ahmad felt that some of the charac-

"Hindustān kī auraton kī hālat" (The Condition of the Women of Hindustan) Khan argues that women have been deprived of *"'ilm kī roshnī"* (the light of knowledge), which has been granted to their male counterparts, who have the opportunity to be educated (Ahmad 155). Sir Syed argues that the education of women would enable them to become good Muslim subjects. To this end, Nazīr Ahmed wrote *Mirāt-ul Urūs* (1869) (*The Bride's Mirror*), a didactic novel which makes explicit the Aligarh reformers' notions of education for women.[12] Ahmad's novel suggests that a "good education" can lead to a woman's social, economic and moral betterment, while a "bad education" can lead a woman to misery and poverty.

teristics of English society—its discipline, order, efficiency and high levels of education, along with science and technology—must be adopted by the Muslim community" (Jones 65).

12 In his introduction to the novel, Nazīr Ahmad writes that "It may be true that 'too much learning is unnecessary for a woman'"(8) but that it is necessary for women to be literate so that they can better manage a household. It is also necessary for them to study the Qur'ān so that they may educate their children at home from the seclusion of *purdāh*. He concludes his introduction by telling his female audience: "And now I am going to tell you an amusing story, which will show you what kind of troubles are brought about by a bad education" (16-17).

In this milieu, Mohammed Hadi Ruswā's *Umrāo Jān Adā* was sensational not only because it portrayed the life of a courtesan rather than that of a *purdāh-nashīn* (veiled) woman, but also because of its unique narrative style, which aimed at realism rather than fantasy or moral didacticism. In the preface to his novel *Zāt-e Sharīf*, Mirzā Ruswā self-consciously draws attention to his attempt to break away from the work of his literary predecessors: "I do not possess the inventive power to delineate events that happened thousands of years ago. Besides, I consider it improper to portray a picture which agrees neither with present day conditions nor with those of the past" (Asaduddin 92).[13]

Most of Ruswā's novels are based on incidents in his own life and those of his fellow contemporaries. For instance, as Fatehpuri notes, the character of Baggan in Ruswā's first novel, *Afshā-e Rāz* (*The Revelation of Secrets*) (1896), is based on his maternal aunt's

---

13 Critics have misread Ruswā's commitment to realist fiction as a commitment to portraying factual events. Thus, there has been much debate in Urdu literary circles about whether Umrāo Jān was indeed based on a real woman by the same name or not; while this is a fascinating historical question it is irrelevant for reading this novel as a literary text.

daughter, Baggan. Ruswā was in love with his cousin and the novel features a romance between two characters, Zaki and Baggan.[14] In this novel, there is mention of Umrāo Jān the courtesan, who is a minor character. Ruswā's next novel, *Umrāo Jān Adā*, features the eponymous protagonist as both narrator and character.

Singer/Poet/Courtesan: The Evolution of Umrāo Jān's Character in Three Novels

There has been much lively debate in literary circles about the historical existence of Umrāo Jān 'Adā,' the person. Some critics have argued that the novel is based on the life of a real woman, while others have maintained that the novel is primarily a work of fiction, which isn't based on historical fact.[15] Through interviews with Ruswā's friends

---

14 In an early essay in *Zamānā* this parallel between Ruswā's work and life is brought to the fore: "[Ruswā] desired to marry his maternal aunt's daughter. *Afshā-e Rāz* or *Gharīb Khāna* [the Poor House], Mirzā's first literary work, largely pertains to their affairs" (Aziz Lucknawi, "Mirzā Ruswā Marh ūm,"*Zamānā*, Kānpūr, January 1933, 5).

15 Fatehpuri has discussed this in detail and has furnished plenty of historical evidence based on archival material. For more details, see "'Umrāo Jān Adā' aur 'Jūnūn-e Intezār'" (pp. 71-85 of *Ruswā Rī Navil Nigan*).

and contemporaries and other archival research, Zaheer Fatehpuri has established that
the character of Umrāo Jān is based on a courtesan by the same name, whom Ruswā was
well-acquainted with. Since we know very
little about Umrāo Jān the person, other than
the fact that she existed, the novels *Afshā-e
Rāz*, *Umrāo Jān Adā* and *Jūnūn-e Intezār* could
serve as possible archives for her history.

In thinking of the novels as historical texts,
we draw on feminist historian Antoinette
Burton's argument that memoirs, letters and
other literary works which have hitherto been
discarded by historians as not adequately
factual can be recuperated as sites of history.[16]
Reading the novels in this vein, to what
extent does Ruswā base his character on the
courtesan, Umrāo Jān? Which elements of
her character does he choose to represent in
his fiction?

In his interviews with Ruswā's students
Murtazā Hussain Musvī and Khādim Abbās,
Fatehpuri establishes that Ruswā was drawn

16 Burton suggests that the act of writing history is itself
modelled on a patriarchal hierarchy of truth (history)
and fiction (literature): "[W]hat women wrote was con-
ventionally designated 'Literature' (the domain of memory, sentiment and fiction) while men claimed the
'objective' task of truth-telling 'History'"(Burton 20).

to Umrāo Jān because of "[her] expertise in the art of music and Mirzā's taste for music" (Fatehpuri 75-76).[17] It is evident from this that Umrāo Jān served as Ruswā's intellectual and perhaps sexual companion. Ruswā's long-term artistic relationship with Umrāo Jān became the basis of his literary depiction of her. While her artistic and literary traits are represented in each novel, there is a gradual evolution of her as a character through successive novels.

In *Afshā-e Rāz* Umrāo Jān is a minor character who appears briefly in the text as a courtesan. In his description of her, Ruswā foregrounds her talents as a singer:

> Mirzā Ruswā had seen Umrāo Jān. He says, 'Ah, Umrāo Jān! God bless her, she was such a discerning woman— she understood people so well. She was dark-skinned, tall, well-groomed and refined in her appearance' ... he [Mirzā Ruswā] said that in those

17 "Mirzā's student Murtazā Hussain Musvī (resident of Mushk Ganj, Lucknow) and Khādim Abbās (resident of Mirān Pūrā, Bāra Ban kī) have shed light on Ruswā's long-term relationship with Umrāo Jān; they believe that the basis of this relationship was Umrāo's expertise in the art of music and Mirzā's taste for music" (Fatehpuri 75-76).

times, he saw several courtesans performing. 'Truly, there has been a lot of progress in the art [of the courtesan], but such difficulties arise that an inexpert singer cannot explicate the nuances of the verse [she sings], but when Umrāo Jān performed, it was easily understood' (*Afshā-e Rāz* 73-74).

In this description, Ruswā differentiates Umrāo Jān from other singers not only through her beauty and her exceptional talent in music, but also through her intelligence: she does not merely parrot poetry, but is able to relay its nuances to a discerning audience. Her mastery over the art of poetry is mentioned, but we do not see evidence of her mastery in the novel, i.e. Umrāo Jān does not compose poetry or participate in a *musha'irā* [a poetry gathering where poets read their poems to an audience]. Our judgment of her skill, then, is based on the narrator Mirzā Ruswā's assessment of her.

In *Umrāo Jān Adā*, Umrāo Jān, the eponymous protagonist of the novel, is a serious *rekhta* composing Urdu poet. *Rekhta*[18] refers to the standard register for Urdu poetry in which poets, irrespective of their gender, adopt a male persona to express desire for a beloved who could be male or female.[19] In the early nineteenth-century another genre of poetry called *rekhtī* was popularised by male Urdu writers. It referred to the adoption of a female voice and the poems written in this genre were usually lewd, licentious accounts of the private affairs of women.[20] Serious Urdu poets, both male and female, from the eighteenth century onwards, only composed poetry in *rekhta*, and *rekhtī* came to be associated primarily with the *begamatī zubān* (women's language) of prostitutes.[21]

18 *Rekhta* literally means "Poured out; scattered; mixed;—s.m. 'The mixed dialect'" (Platts 611). It refers to a particular kind of poetry using a "mix" of Hindi (read Urdu) and Persian linguistic features. *Rekhta* also referred to the language Hindi/Urdu until the last quarter of the nineteenth century.

19 "In the 'Persian' mode, the poet uses a masculine voice for himself, and addresses a beloved who could be male or female. (This mode later gained exclusive dominance in the Urdu *ghazal* in all parts of India.) In the 'Indic' mode, on the other hand, the poet/lover adopts a feminine voice for himself, while addressing a beloved who is always male" (Naim 6). For more details on this see C.M. Naim's "Transvestic Words: The *Rekhtī* in Urdu."

20 In her essay on *rekhtī*, Carla Petievich argues that *rekhtī* belittled women by representing their experiences in ribald and licentious terms and by creating poems in a conversational Urdu register, which far differed from the formal register of *rekhtā*.

21 "It was into this milieu that *rekhtī* was introduced by Sa'dat Yar Khan 'Rangīn' (1756-1834), the son of a

Ruswā is at pains to differentiate Umrāo Jān's skill in poetry from that of other prostitutes at the very outset. The novel starts with a *musha'irā*, in which a group of men gather to recite poetry. Mirzā Ruswā, the narrator, is among them and he recites a *sh'er* (a mono-rhymed two-line verse) to the acclaim of his male audience. Umrāo Jān overhears him and exclaims her approval, and she is subsequently invited to join the *musha'irā*. Umrāo Jān is called upon by her audience to recite a *sh'er*:

> *kā'abe main jā ke bhūl gayā rāh dair kī*
> *īman bach gayā mere maulā ne kher kī*
> (Ruswā 're')

> On my visit to the Ka'abā I forgot
> the road to the Church

Persian nobleman who had migrated to Lucknow around the turn of the nineteenth century. By way of introduction to his literary innovation, Rangīn explains that, in the course of a wild and mis-spent youth, he consorted extensively with the famous courtesans of the day. In their company he developed familiarity with and appreciation of their particular idiom. The pithiness of their expression and their wit so impressed him that he decided to compose poetry in this 'Ladies' Language' (*begamatī zubān*) and to call his collected poems '*rekhtī*'. The combination of its feminine narrator and its *begamatī* idiom made *rekhtī* a distinct genre. Indications are that this immediately-popular style of poetry was accepted quite unproblematically into Lucknow's thriving milieu" (Petievich 78).

My faith was saved, my Lord was merciful

In this couplet, Umrāo Jān assumes the normative male voice of *rekhta* rather than the feminine voice of *rekhtī*. Umrāo Jān uses a masculine verb ending to represent herself. In response to this poem, Khan Sahab, one of the connoisseurs of poetry present, questions her use of the male voice in the verse. An incensed Umrāo Jān asks Khan Sahab whether he thinks she is only capable of composing *rekhtī*. Khan Sahab responds by saying that only *rekhtī* befits a woman. Khan Sahab's attempt to pigeon-hole Umrāo Jān into a *rekhtī* composing poet on account of her gender and her profession meets with hostility from Umrāo Jān because she considers herself a serious poet, and as a serious poet she naturally assumes the normative male voice in her poetic compositions. Furthermore the subject of the verse is Islamic piety rather than the sexual adventures of women.

Through the course of the novel, we are introduced to Umrāo Jān's various talents—not only does she compose poetry, she is also invited to sing *marsīyahs* (elegies written for Husayn and his companions martyred at Karbalā) and to dance for the landed gentry.

We learn of these talents through Umrāo Jān's narration of her life story—she is an accomplished storyteller. However, this is not a skill that Umrāo Jān wants to be known for. At the end of *Umrāo Jān Adā*, Mirzā Ruswā informs the reader that Umrāo Jān was incensed when she learnt that Ruswā had committed her memoirs to paper and had published them as a novel. This then becomes the pretext for *Jūnūn-e Intezār Yā'nī Fasāna'-e Mirzā Ruswā* (*The Madness of Waiting: The story of Mirzā Ruswā*). The first edition of *Umrāo Jān Adā* advertises *Jūnūn-e Intezār* on the back cover and claims that the latter is penned by Umrāo Jān herself.[22]

While we have evidence suggesting that Umrāo Jān was indeed a real person, it is unlikely that she has penned the novella for two reasons. First, although *Junūn-e Intezār* was published with Umrāo Jān Adā as the author (March, 1899), its date of publication is printed as April 1 1899, All Fool's Day. This clearly suggests that the novella is a prank. Second, large sections of the *mathnavī Nāla'-*

22 "*Jūnūn-e Intezār Yā'nī Fasāna'-e Mirzā Ruswā*, authored by Umrāo Jān Adā. Whoever Sire reads Umrāo Jān Adā should kindly look at this as well. It consists of *mathnavī* 'Nāla'-e Ruswā' which is so terrific that the reader will definitely appreciate it. Price, nothing; just 2 . . ." (Fatehpuri 90-91).

e Ruswā (*The Lament of Ruswā*), embedded in *Jūnūn-e Intezār*, are similar in tone and theme to *Ummīd-o Bīm* [Hope and Fear], an earlier *mathnavī* by Ruswā. *Ummīd-o Bīm* is a wide-ranging treatise on human aspirations and desires, divided into three sections: in the first section, *Ishq-e Tāzā* (New Love), Ruswā narrates the details of his love affair with a European woman who studied at Isabella Thobern College in Lucknow.[23] Since this text is lost, there is no evidence that the woman referred to in these verses is Sophia, the protagonist of *Nāla'-e Ruswā*. However, a few stray verses recorded in Fatehpuri's book are thematically and linguistically similar to verses in *Nāla'-e Ruswā*, which pertain to Ruswā's affair with Sophia. They also have the same metrical structure:[24]

23 Fatehpuri documents that Aziz Lucknawai (a contemporary of Ruswā) was of the belief that "*Ishq-e Tāzā*," a section of *Ummīd-o Bīm*, was devoted to Ruswā's affair with a 'farangan' (foreigner, usually a term applied to Europeans). Fatehpuri quoting Lucknawi's essay writes: "During his employment at the Women's College he fell madly in love with a European woman. This gifted beloved has also been shrewdly named at some place in this *mathnavī* by arranging verses so that the initials of the lines being put together may form the name" ("Mirzā Ki Sha'irī," *Zamānā* Kānpūr, April 1933.)

24 In Urdu poetry the metrical system is based on vowels classified as either 'long' or 'short.' In a *ghazal*, *mathnavī*, or any other structured form of verse in Urdu poetry, all the verses in a poem follow a single meter. For

Ishq-e Tāzā
Kion churatey ho nazar dekho tou!
Jhainpte kiā ho, idhar dekho tou!

Chāhte ho tum agar merī falāh
Kion kisī shakhs se lete hou salāh

Why do you avert your gaze, do
   look here!
Don't shy away, do look here!

If you desire my welfare
Why take advice from another

Jūnūn
dil main kuch khauf-e vālidain na thā
mere dekhe baġhair chain na thā

donon ke dil main chor agar hotā
kion na hum ko kisī kādar hotā

wāqa'i jab dilon main safāī hotī hai tou
   ankhain kabhī nahīn jhainptīn.

jab na ho kuch tou dil main shak kion ho
milne julne main phir jhijak kion ho

There was no fear of parents
Without seeing me she had no repose

If both of us thought we were erring

example, in the *mathnavī Nāla'-e Ruswā*, all the verses of
all the *sh'ers* have the same meter consisting of ten syl-
lables. The metrical structure of the *mathnavī Ummīd-o
Bīm* is the same.

Why wouldn't we have feared society

Truly, when the heart is pure, there is no
need to lower one's eyes in shame.

When there is nothing wrong,
why should the heart fear?
Why then should there be any hesitation
in meeting?

The verses in both *Ishq-e Tāzā* and *Nāla-e Ruswā* urge the lover to defy societal norms and reaffirm his passion for the beloved, and we know that both texts delineate an interracial relationship. *Jūnūn-e Intezār*'s indebtedness to *Ummīd-o Bīm* clearly establishes Ruswā and not Umrāo Jān as the author of this text.

Through this brief overview of the three texts, we see the evolution of Ruswā's representation of Umrāo Jān's character: from an accomplished singer in *Afshā-e Rāz*, to a *rekhta* composing poet in *Umrāo Jān*, and finally as author in *Jūnūn-e Intezār*. In contrast, all we know about Umrāo Jān the person is the fact that she is an accomplished singer. The representation of Umrāo Jān in Ruswā's fiction suggests the possibility that she was also a poet and a writer.[25] Umrāo Jān's character,

25 There is debate in literary circles about whether it is possible that Umrāo Jān, the woman, was responsible

then, represents the multiple possibilities of artistic expression available to women at this historical moment.

Recovering a Feminist Voice:
A Journey through Text and Archive

Umrāo Jān's significance as a historical character raises the question of whether we can recover her story for the feminist archive in the same way that feminist historians have sought to recover women's narratives from historical and legal documents. In her study of sixteenth century women's legal narratives, feminist historian Natalie Zemon Davis argues that the 'literary' aspects of a historical document can enable a richer understanding of the history contained in it. She writes: "I want to let the 'fictional' aspects of these documents be the centre of analysis. By 'fictional' I do not mean their feigned elements, but rather, using the other broader sense of the root word *fingere*, their forming,

for some of the verses that appear in Ruswa's novels. However, Fatehpuri has established that the poetry associated with her character in the novel *Umrāo Jān Adā* has been composed by Ruswā himself (Aziz Lucknawi, "Mirzā Ruswā Marhūm," *Zamānā*, Kānpūr, January 1933; Ali Abbas Hussain and Mumtaz Hussain Jonpuri's interviews as cited in Fatehpuri).

shaping and molding elements: the crafting of a narrative" (Davis 3). Davis suggests that the narrative form of history, its literary structure, informs its contents.

Just as Davis rethinks the genre of history in the context of its 'literariness,' we similarly rethink the genre of 'literature' in terms of its 'historicity.' As discussed above, large parts of *Umrāo Jān Adā* and *Jūnūn-e Intezār* are informed by contemporary histories such as the *Qaisar al Tawārīkh*, so in a sense both are historical novels. We seek to determine a slightly different relation here: can the text of *Jūnūn-e Intezār* serve as a historical archive for the lost history of Umrāo Jān, the character, author, narrator and woman? Can we recover a feminist voice by reading Umrāo Jān through layers of textual narration?

Feminist historians have suggested that the historical archive for women is located in the construct of home, as women write their narratives through and to the home. Burton explains the significance of the home for women: "I want to emphasize, in other words, the importance of home as both a material archive for history and a very real political figure in an extended moment of historical crisis" (Burton 5). How does Umrāo

Jān negotiate her space within the material archive of 'home' as narrator and character? To understand this it is necessary first to understand the valences of home in colonial and reformist discourse at this historical moment.

Colonial discourse produced the *zenānā* (women's quarter) as the 'harem'—a confining space in which the veiled woman led a blighted life.[26] Unveiled women who lived outside the home in the *kothā* (brothel) represented the dark, illicit mysteries of the East. The "nautch girl" epitomized this construct, and the "civilizing" mission in this context involved disciplining the sexuality of courtesans and other "disreputable" women in new ways. In contrast, social reformers argued that the veiled woman's inhabitation of the home protected her from the evils of the colonial public sphere and enabled her

26 An American feminist, Katherine Mayo, strove to "civilise" the *purdāh-nashīn* woman by stripping her of her veil and bringing her into the public sphere. In this case, the existence of *purdāh* justified the "civilizing" mission of colonialism. Inderpal Grewal argues that in the South Asian context, "The *'purdāh'* [veil] construct of the English imperialists becomes the 'home' of the Indian nationalists" (Grewal 54), i.e. the opacity of the veiled woman to the Orientalist gaze was produced by the nationalists as essential for preserving her modesty and maintaining her respectability.

جُوْن‌اں

to become a "guardian of orthodoxy" who could preserve Islamic culture for the Muslim man.[27] In this context, the *kothā* took on the eroticized elements of the *zenānā* and became the socially sanctioned counterpoint to the women's quarters of the respectable home for the reformers.

Where do we place Umrāo Jān in the dichotomy produced between *zenānā* and *kothā* by both imperialists and social reformers? We suggest that Umrāo Jān belongs neither to the *zenānā* nor to the *kothā*; rather, she exists in a liminal space between the two worlds. This liminal space is both a physical structure—the not-quite respectable 'home'— and an abstract construct of femininity.

In *Umrāo Jān Adā*, Umrāo Jān's home is gestured to as a shadowy space, populated by its mistress and her servants, but never

27 Note, this construction of the inner-sphere and the outer-sphere is similar to that created by Bengali nationalists at the turn of the century. As Partha Chatterjee argues in *The Nation and its Fragments*, colonialism compelled the Bengali middle-class male to conceive of the world as separated into a material 'outer' world and a spiritual 'inner' world. While men struggled in the material outer world against Western influences, they were safe in the knowledge that women guarded the spiritual inner world of the *bhadralok* home and maintained it as a hallowed sanctuary for them.

specifically described. As we learn from the introduction to the novel, this home is not located in the *bāzār-e-husn* or courtesans' quarters, but rather in the midst of a *sharīf* [respectable] locality. Umrāo Jān does not make her presence known in this locality for fear of ostracism. For the duration of the novel, she remains in a single room with Ruswā, recounting her life story. The story of her life, however, sweeps the reader away from the confines of her room, as Umrāo Jān travels both within the city of Lucknow and between cities of the United Provinces (present-day Uttar Pradesh). This travel is enabled and necessitated by her profession as a courtesan, and would have been deemed both impossible and inappropriate for any veiled woman.

This juxtaposition of the stationary narrative present, in which Umrāo Jān is located firmly in a habitus, with the peripatetic past, in which 'home' is not a space but a location of memory/archive, suggests that Umrāo Jān's inhabitation (however precarious) of the material home enables her to narrate home as archive. And it is in narration and in the site of narration that the home is also reconfigured as a locus for the political. For the act of narration is premised on the notion of the home as the private sphere, and the narration commences on this assumption—Umrāo Jān believes that Ruswā will not make public the details of her life. In this, Umrāo Jān locates herself squarely in the narrative of the private/public which structures the life of the veiled woman.

In exposing Umrāo Jān's life by publishing the novel, which itself becomes a record of the archive (albeit a self-referential one), Ruswā violates the private/public distinction that Umrāo Jān holds to. Consequently, in *Jūnūn-e Intezār*, Umrāo Jān is compelled to move out of the private—the material home and the historical archive of memory—to avenge herself. In the preface to the novella, she tells the reader that Ruswā has disgraced her by publishing the memoirs of her life without her permission in *Umrāo Jān Adā*, and that the following text is an attempt to avenge herself. Umrāo Jān, whom the reader knows as a poet of some renown from *Umrāo Jān Adā*, frames her threat to avenge herself in poetry:

Dushnām dey key mujhko bohat khush na ho jiyey
Kiā kījiyeygā āp jo merī zubān khulī

Be not too contented, having defamed
me just so,
What would you do, if my tongue
becomes a bit looser like yours?

In this verse, Umrāo Jān states that
Mirzā Ruswā has 'defamed' her by publishing
her story because he has made public the
intimate details of her life and in doing so
has ruined her reputation. This is made more
explicit in the next verse when she threatens
to avenge herself by 'loosening her tongue,'
i.e. by revealing the intimate details of Mirzā
Ruswā's life. This prefatory note establishes
Umrāo Jān as the 'narrator' of the text.

However, almost immediately after introducing Umrāo Jān as the narrator of this text,
Ruswā robs her of this role through the
narrative device of the *mathnavī Nāla'-e Ruswā*.
The text of *Jūnūn-e Intezār* is for the most part
the text of the *mathnavī Nāla'-e Ruswā* with
occasional interjections by Umrāo Jān. In
these interjections, Umrāo Jān reminds the
reader time and again that she is revealing
private information about Mirzā Ruswā's life,
which he would rather not have made

28 "Ever since he decided to publish my biography, I
vowed that I would reveal a few of his secrets to the
world" (*Jūnūn-e Intezār*; Ruswa 1).

public.[28] In doing so, she overlays Mirzā Ruswā's narrative voice with her own, subtly undermining his authority as the author of the text. Through this move, Umrāo Jān establishes herself as a speaking subject who defends herself against her public humiliation at the hands of Mirzā Ruswā.

However, the layered narrative structure of this text shields her from the direct gaze of the reader through the elaborate artifice of the *mathnavī*, for it is not her but the *mathnavī* which exposes the intimate details of Mirzā Ruswā's life. Once again, the voice of the speaking subject, Umrāo Jān, is modulated by Mirzā Ruswā, the narrator of *Umrāo Jān Adā*, who is now also a character in this story. Therefore, through this text, Umrāo Jān defends herself against accusations of immodesty both through her own textual interjections and through the narrative structure of the text itself. The contradiction between Umrāo Jān's position as narrator and her desires as a character are thus resolved through the metaphoric narrative veil. In other words, the narrative veil enables Umrāo Jān to 'author' the text while still maintaining the 'home' as the space of the private.

The paradoxes of Umrāo Jān's position—her desire to inhabit the home, the archive of the *purdāh-nashīn* woman and her inability to fully do so—represent her liminality as character, 'author' and narrator. She is simultaneously relegated to the margin of the narrative and to the worlds of the *zenānā* and *kothā*. In recovering her voice, then, we also recover the contradictory narrative of a modesty-desiring courtesan, whose voice has been subsumed by dominant imperial and reformist discourse, which figure the courtesan as necessarily licentious and the 'other' to the pristine veiled woman. More broadly, the text of *Jūnūn-e Intezār* becomes a site for the feminist archive both materially and politically. The text is a material archive that 'houses' the desires of a courtesan who cannot be accommodated within dominant narratives of respectability that are part of the political context of her time. From a feminist perspective, the text of *Jūnūn-e Intezār* is an archive not only in the sense of a history, a memory, but also a literary work whose narrative strategies compel us to rethink the ways in which we read and write women's voices.

In this respect, *Jūnūn-e Intezār* provides a critical intervention in the study of the

late-nineteenth century courtesan in South
Asia. Since the figure of Umrāo Jān has been
central to these explorations, this text ex-
plores another dimension of Umrāo Jān's
voice, one that has not been visible since the
original publication of the novella. Although
we can never know which aspects of Umrāo
Jān's character are fictional and which
historical, her charisma as a literary figure is
undeniable. The fact that the novel *Umrāo Jān
Adā* is still widely read and circulated
through various media testifies to Umrāo
Jān's enduring hold on the South Asian imagination and Ruswā's literary talent. It is with
genuine excitement and pleasure that we
introduce *Jūnūn-e Intezār* in English translation for the first time and hope that it will
survive another age.

WORKS CITED

ASADUDDIN, M. "First Urdu Novel: Contesting Claims And Disclaimers." *Annual Of Urdu Studies* 16.i (2001): 76-97. *Index Islamicus*. Web. 3 Jun. 2007.

BURTON, Antoinette M. *Dwelling in the Archive: Women Writing House, Home, and History in Late Colonial India.* Oxford: Oxford University Press, 2003. Print.

CHATTERJEE, Partha. *The Nation and Its Fragments: Colonial and Postcolonial Histories.* Delhi: Oxford University Press, 1995. Print.

DAVIS, Natalie Zemon. *Fiction in the Archives: Pardon Tales and Their Tellers in Sixteenth-Century France.* Stanford: Stanford University Press, 1990. Print.

FATEHPURI, Zaheer. *Ruswā Kī Nāvil Nigārī.* Rawalpindi: Horūf, 1970.

GREWAL, Inderpal. *Home and Harem: Nation, Gender, Empire, and the Cultures of Travel.* Durham: Duke UP, 1996. Print.

JONES, Kenneth W. *The New Cambridge History of India: Socio-religious Reform Movements in British India.* Cambridge: Cambridge University Press, 1989. Print.

NAIM, C. M. "Transvestic Words? The Rekhti In Urdu." *Annual Of Urdu Studies* 16.(2001): 3-26. *MLA International Bibliography*. Web. 3 Jun. 2007.

PETIEVICH, Carla. "Rekhti: Impersonating the Feminine in Urdu Poetry." *Sexual Sites, Seminal Attitudes: Sexualities, Masculinities, and Culture in South Asia.* By Sanjay Srivastava. New Delhi: Sage, 2004. 123-146 . Print.

PLATTS, John T. *A Dictionary of Urdū, Classical Hindī, and English.* Whitefish: Kessinger, 2004. Print.

PRITCHETT, Frances W. *Nets of Awareness: Urdu Poetry and Its Critics.* Berkeley: University of California, 1994. Web. 3 Jan. 2011.

THE MADNESS OF WAITING

Dear Reader,

You may have read the story of my life published by Mirzā Ruswā. I am not one to pronounce judgment on him. I won't declare whether he did a good thing or a bad thing, but let us just say that had I known that he would publish the story of my waywardness I would never have narrated it to him. Mirzā Ruswā must have cast a spell on me. Perhaps the most amusing part of this story is that he thinks he has done me a favour by publishing my biography. If indeed this is a "favour" then I know well how it must be returned.

"Mirzā Sāhib, don't be too pleased with yourself for having ruined my reputation. I wonder what you will do if my tongue is loosened?"

Reader, let me tell you that it was not easy to investigate the circumstances of Mirzā Ruswā's life because he is the kind of man who hides from people. In addition, he lives in a place which is difficult to access. I have only had the honour of visiting him once, but at a time when I knew he would not be at home. The reason is that ever since he decided to publish my biography, I vowed that I would reveal a few of his secrets to the world, and I have had to make special arrangements for doing so. I did this by making one of his servants (whose name and address I cannot of course reveal) my accomplice.

One day, when Mirzā Sāhib was attending a *mushā'ira*[1] at a friend's place, I immediately hired a car and went to his house. His servant (the one who was my accomplice) showed me each and every corner of his house. Thanks to this man, I found one of Mirzā Sāhib's books which contained a photo, some letters and an incomplete manuscript of a *maśnavī*,[2] Nālā-e Ruswā. In the course of my investigation, I also gleaned some information about him from his friends. I collated all my research and published it as a novella. The day that Mirzā Ruswā published my biography and sent a copy for my perusal, on that very day I sent him a copy of this short piece of prose. I am sure Mirzā Ruswā is not happy about this, but what else could I have done?

Devotedly
Umrāo Jān Adā.

1st April 1899

1 An informal gathering where poets recite original compositions.

2 A *maśnavī* is a long narrative poem in which two half-lines of each verse correspond in meter, which remains the same throughout the poem. Also in each verse, both half-lines end in the same rhyme, which can change from verse to verse. It is of the following form:
——a ——a
——b ——b

Junūn-e Intezār
Ya'nī
Fasānā-e Mirzā Ruswā

One should be beautiful and good natured
For what else does a human being need?

There is much charm in Mirzā Ruswā's dignified comportment and eloquent speech
for both women and men are drawn to him
at every gathering. Whenever he speaks,
people listen to him with concentration. No
matter how sad one may be, one's sadness
dissipates after a few moments in Mirzā
Ruswā's presence. His wit can make even a
crying man laugh. His God given intelligence,
his amazing knowledge and experience
augment his fine personality. His affinity for
poetry and words is complemented by his
refined taste in beauty. These attributes however, are tempered by bouts of insanity. A few
doctors surmise that his fainting spells are
due to his maddened state of mind. Some

think that he has been charmed into a fantasy world of fairies. There is certainly something mysterious about Mirzā Sāhib.

One of Mirzā Sāhib's close friends, let's suppose it is me, has composed a poem extolling his virtues. It is written in the same metre as his *maśnavī* Nālā-e Ruswā. Here it is:[3]

"One of my good friends Ruswā, having left his hearth and home, wanders crazed in the streets. He lives in a state of perpetual madness because the poor soul lost his heart. As a traveller on the highway of failure, his journey leads him only to oblivion. His heart is restless and without peace, his body sick because he is without food or sleep. Mirzā Sāhib has become the leader of faithful lovers, those who desire self-annihilation and self-mortification. He has been killed by the sword of intimacy and arrows of unfulfilled desires for his lover are his executioner. Now his crazed mind is intent upon its own destruction, and has lost all sense of propriety.

"He is wracked with unfulfilled desires and tormented by anxiety, and his stunned heart has become indifferent. He is sleepless, devoid even of dreams, while his restless heart is devoid of peace. He sheds torrents of tears, each eyelash unleashes streams of blood. And while each teardrop is crimson his visage is yellow and pale. His lips are parched and all he can do is sigh and chant the name of his beloved like an incantation. In short, we can surmise that Mirzā Sāhib's heart has been trapped by someone. Mirzā Sāhib loves an infidel and has sacrificed his faith and beliefs to her. He is my friend, but what can I say to him? The truth is that a madness is upon him. To die for someone in this way, to love with such intensity the beloved who is the enemy of your life is surely insanity. Sir, it is in this way that the heart wastes away. The heart can find repose only if one is sensible and does not die of adoration. His love has crossed all boundaries and he is in a terrible state."

"Enough! You must leave this madness, abandon your love at once. Mirzā Sāhib, why for god's sake do you die for love and that too for the love of the unfaithful beloved? What can be gained from your unfulfilled desires and wishes? What can be gained from your unreasonable waiting for her return? Nothing will be gained by simply proclaiming that your waiting is an injustice. Nor will anything be gained by your sighing and pleading. What do you hope to gain from your impossible desire to meet her? Love which requires patience is unyielding. In this situation, complaining of your failure is pointless."

"Alas! One as intelligent and wise as you sits and mopes like a hopeless lover! If there is nothing wrong with your mind, why don't you take the advice of the practical (one)?[4] I say all this unwillingly—do forgive me. For other than this madness you are a collection of virtues—a jester, witty and charming. You are a master of enchantment and of coquetry. You are a poet who not only measures his eloquent words, but is also judicious and refined in his taste."

"Who but Mirzā Sāhib has acquired such refined taste? He is a brilliant writer. He is quick-witted, and his diction is impeccable. He excels at writing and is therefore in command of literary battles, social gatherings and of course of sentences and all forms of poetry. The truth is that Mirzā Ruswā's expertise in poetry makes him a wonderful conversationalist. Why then shouldn't he be the darling of art connoisseurs?"

"He is detached from success and abstains from proclaiming himself since he has no desire for fame or admirers. Have you ever met

4 We know that the poet of these verses is a woman because in Urdu the gender for "I" in these verses is feminine. From this we can infer that Umrāo Jān, the narrator-character, has written this poem.

anyone like him? Mirzā Sāhib does not mingle with just anybody. However, when he does pause to meet someone he greets them with warmth. Mirzā Sāhib is pure, his character pristine. He is handsome and well-disposed. There is subtlety in every conversation and delicacy in every verse."

"His conduct is dignified, splendid and valorous. Although he has pride, authority and gravity, when required he also behaves with humility. His conduct is wise and he acts always with compassion. He follows the laws of the Prophet with his heart and he is therefore always true to his principles. He is simple and open-hearted. Even though it may not be apparent to others, one should never waver in one's faith to god because the body is connected to the soul and the heart to belief. There is nothing but goodness in his soul and he is therefore always agreeable and makes no enemies."

"He cannot stand the treachery of hypocrites and has no patience for lewd conversation. He whole-heartedly despises slyness and hates those who make hasty judgments. There is no formality in his demeanor, nor any prejudice in his nature. He is not acquainted with evil and has no knowledge of malice and obstinacy. He is never annoyed by quibblers and does not fight with them. He is frank with his companions and is not fond of bombast."

"His favour to me is itself a sign of his kindness. I am devoted to him and proud of my devotion. His favour to me has made me respectable in my own eyes. Otherwise what am I, what is my stature? Of what significance is my self and my nature?"[5]

5 Here ends the poem that Umrāo Jān claims is composed by one of Mirzā Sāhib's friends.

"Why ask the whereabouts of a crazed one like me?

I find peace only in the city of madness"

I have composed this just as Mirzā Sāhib would have. In truth, the place where he lives should be called the city of madness—it is two miles (kos) from Lucknow, next to the road that leads to Nawāb-Ganj by the iron bridge. One can see four squat walls that enclose a garden. The garden is surrounded by miles of open field. There is no sign of human inhabitation anywhere. Some time ago, there were quite a few travellers on this road. However, ever since the railroad has been laid this way, human traffic has decreased on this road. In this wilderness, Mirzā Sāhib finds repose. He lives here with two or three servants. In the centre of his garden lies a pleasant little cottage. In front of the cottage at a little distance lies a round, concrete terrace which is surrounded by the garden. This is the place where he sits all day and night. In the north corner of this garden, there is an area skirted by a wooden fence in which there are mounds of stones. Strange and marvelous trees have been laid atop these stones in such a way that it seems that the trees grow from the stones. In the centre of this is a white marble pool filled with water. Small canals of water radiate in all four directions from this pool. This area is protected from sunlight by reed mats. In the hot summer days it is cool here because several water-carriers continuously splash this place with water. Mirzā Sāhib often sits here in the afternoon. This is the perfect place for repose and poetry. The rooms of the cottage are well decorated. Mirzā Sāhib lives in one of these rooms. The others remain locked.

In the *maśnavī Nālā-e Ruswā* , Ruswā Sāhib himself has composed the following verses on the state of this cottage:

"I suffer the agony of waiting in this cottage where I live. Once there lived here a gentleman who was intelligent, wise and noble. He was fond of the realm of wisdom and had a taste for the finer points of nature."

In one of the rooms of this cottage, which the servant unlocked for me, I saw six or seven cupboards filled with books in English.

In front of the cottage is a little hut, which is surrounded on all four sides by an iron grill in which all kinds of instruments have been fitted. The manservant explained that these instruments indicate weather conditions: heat, cold, storms, rain, earthquakes etc. In one corner, I saw a very deep well which has a tall tower made from iron pillars atop it. A dense darkness shrouds both the well and the tall tower so that a lantern is necessary even in broad daylight. There are holes in the frame of this tower, through which one can see stars in the daylight. By the well there is a small concrete cottage. There are many large binoculars in this cottage as well as two globes and some other things with which I am unfamiliar. Mirzā Sāhib writes the following about the person who owns this garden and this cottage.

"He had a beautiful fairy-like daughter whose beauty overshone that of the sun and the moon. How do I describe her beautiful face? Let us just say that she was as lovely as this image."

By good fortune I happened to come across the photograph he was referring to. But Mirzā Sāhib begged me to return it to him otherwise I would willingly have shared a copy of it with you.

"Look! Isn't this a wonderful face? It is the face that has spelt my death. The one you behold is the murderer of my wretched soul and the executioner of my heart. I have never seen such treacherous glances nor have I seen anyone as cruel. Alas! I love her for this coquetry, I love this adorable one. Don't say anything; my heart is convinced that she is adorable."

There is no doubt that she is adorable. I appreciate Mirzā Sāhib's discerning taste.

"She is indeed adorable. Behold these half closed eyes, the beguiling bashfulness of her glances. It is these eyes which have caused this affliction, these tresses which have arrested me. Behold the spell her eyebrows cast, the bewitchment of her glances. Her attraction is unique, her affection has flair. Behold her dazzling smile and contemplate the eloquence of her speech. What can I say about her pleasant speech? There is no way I can render in words the charm of her coquetry."

The verses that Mirzā Ruswā has written on the eloquence of her speech are truly worthy of praise. For he has rendered them with much refinement.

"When it is difficult even to take a photograph of her, how then can my thoughts or my imagination reach her? What can be said about the delicacy of the speech of the one whose beauty cannot be rendered by a photograph? If only the photograph would speak and reveal to us the mysteries of her speech! By what means can I make her speak? Alas! The eloquence of her speech remains only in these few letters."

All of these letters are in English, but I have translated some of them into Urdu, for your convenience. From these letters we can confirm that Mirzā Ruswā's statements about her are true. The idiom is absolutely clear, but this simplicity is not without formality. Each word is suffused with meaning and each sentence is in eloquent English. I wish that I were able to write such fine prose in Urdu.

THE MADNESS OF WAITING

"Behold the charm of these words! Look at how wonderful these sentences are. Reader! Be the judge of these words—have you ever seen such prose? What shall I say? I have read these letters a hundred times, and I am incapable of judging them. Now you tell me if they contain any unnecessary words. The prose is colourful and utterly magical! Have I ever written a word so eloquent? I have written about everything, but none of my words amount to anything in comparison!"

This was Mirzā Sāhib's description of her writing style. Now I will narrate his description of her speech. Mirzā Ruswā has composed wonderful poetry to explicate this, as well.

"Her speech and accent are beautiful, and the fire of her voice is fiercer than lightning. She has a lilt in her voice. She is naturally disposed to tune and euphony. Her voice is as melodious as though it were trained by some master musician and as if the melody emanates from her otherwise cunning heart."

This verse and the two or three verses after it can only be understood by someone who is well-versed in of the art of music.

"Every word she speaks is well-considered, every action well-thought out, and likewise her disposition too is well-balanced. She

53

carries herself with poise and her tresses are never entangled. Her gait is never clumsy. Her soft foot-prints are delicate, her petite frame devastatingly beautiful."

The verse after this one reveals that the woman was of fair complexion. Europeans are of fair complexion. But it's difficult to discern this from her photograph.

"What a rosy and fair complexion she had, and this in combination with her coquetry was simply bewitching. All the fair ones I have seen until now are bland and dull. There is no brilliance in them. They do not have the charm of this fairy."

Truly, beloveds of a fair complexion are dull. Those who have both brilliance and dignity and also flair and gravity are rarely to be seen. Mirzā Sāhib tells us the following about the pedigree of this Miss Sāhiba.

"Miss Sāhiba's paternal grandfather was a Frenchman and her maternal grandfather was a Londoner. However, both her parents were born in India and loved this country from the bottom of their hearts."

Miss Sāhiba herself was born in Lucknow. The date of her birth was inscribed at the back of the photograph, but unfortunately I forgot to write it down.

"She herself was born in Lucknow and was raised in this city. Her wet nurse and her nanny were both from Lucknow too."

Although her mother tongue was English—

"She spoke pristine Urdu that was both idiomatic and clear! She never stammered, and her speech was never incoherent."

It's unfortunate that we don't have a single specimen of her Urdu with us. In my life, I have rarely heard a white man or woman speak idiomatic Urdu, but I happily accept this to be true based on Mirzā Sāhib's testament. If this is true then Miss Sāhiba's intelligence is indeed worthy of praise.

"Although she was always polite, her speech was nevertheless full of wit."

Mirzā Ruswā suggests that the following circumstances nurtured his relationship with Miss Sāhiba:

"My famous and respected uncle, who is well-known throughout the city was a commander in the royal army."

I would have written his uncle's name here, but doing so would be very discourteous to Mirzā Sāhib.

"Miss Sāhiba's father was indebted to him because he saved his life from enemies during the Mutiny by giving him shelter in his house. It is evident that her father lived in tenuous circumstances, but he nevertheless lived happily in his home. His womenfolk and ours grew close. It became a well-established custom that a lady from his home would visit our house and my aunt would sometimes go to their house. The men went back and forth every day and gifts were always exchanged between the houses. The lady of his house was virtuous at heart and on every important occasion she would send a cake. This sentence is fit for a poem. Your aunt would in turn cook *sevayyāň*[6] and send it to her. She would celebrate Eid at home and send sweets to their house. Flowers would arrive from Miss Sāhiba's garden and my aunt would likewise send jujubes from the fruit trees in her garden."

6 A rice based dessert served especially on the occasion of Eid.

Mirzā Ruswā has truncated this verse and turned it into another verse which I write below. I think however, that the real pleasure is in the original verse.

"Flowers would come from their garden and my aunt would send mangoes from her grove."

It is possible that mangoes would go from her garden, but sending jujubes from the ju-

jube tree in the small courtyard of her home shows the extreme courtesy and sincerity of such a gesture which befits the natural disposition of us women.[7]

"This custom had been going on for ages, and what a wonderful neighbourly courtesy it was. There was genuine affection among the older generation."

There is no doubt that examples of true love were common among our ancestors, and that our world is now more selfish.

"Although religion forbade their love, theirs was nevertheless a pure love."

Despite the freedom we have these days to follow our own religion and despite the abandonment of various traditions of the *Sharia*,[8] religious prejudice is even more evident these days than it was then.

"He was Muslim, she was Christian, but there were no misgivings in their hearts. They were not aware of religious prejudice and they refused to believe in such things. It was impossible for them to think about religion as a divisive force just as it was impossible for them to hurt anyone. Such people are long gone. How terrible that people like them do not exist any more."

7 The narrator makes this comment probably because she considers mangoes commonplace and accords jujubes greater value.

8 Islamic law.

Mirzā Ruswā and Miss Sāhiba played together in their childhood, and they fell in love with each other when they were still children. Mirzā Ruswā narrated this event in the following verses:

"In those days of chivalry and romance, when love was possible I became intimate with Sofia and by and by, my mad yearning for her increased. Our intimacy and attachment exceeded all bounds. In this way, my delicate heart was taken captive by her, and in time a madness came upon me."

But this love was not one-sided. True disinterested love can never be one-sided.

"In short, such was my intimacy with the one who held my life in her hands that she and I were both restless without each other. We could think of nothing other than each other, and we could not think of our love in moral terms."

Such is the nature of childhood love. But the problem was that one was male and the other female. Such love naturally leads to a predictable conclusion. But in those days,

"There was no fear of parents. Without seeing me she had no repose. If both of us thought we were erring, we would have feared society. However, when there is nothing wrong, there is no reason for the heart to fear. Why then should there be any hesitation in meeting each other?"

Truly, when the heart is pure, there is no need to lower one's eyes in shame.

"Our love was true, our intimacy pure. Her love exceeded mine. How well I remember those days of boyhood and mischief and of course of joyous pleasure. Alas! When I remember those days today, it is with a heavy heart."

Soon after, both families were ruined by death. Mirzā Ruswā's paternal uncle died and a few days later his aunt died, as well. It would be better to hear of this incident in Mirzā Ruswā's words:

"When my uncle died I was completely distraught. He had cared for me since childhood And I had become an adult in his care. His love for me was boundless and I loved him very much as well. Then my aunt died, as well. Indeed, death does not spare anyone."

This was the state of his house. Listen to what happened in the other house:

"In this period, the Englishman departed from this world. His wife too had passed away and thus, Sofia was alone in her house. In short, both my house and hers were destroyed by death."

Unfortunately, Mirzā Ruswā could not even pay his condolences for the following reasons.

"Although it was expected that I would go and pay my condolences, a few circumstances made it inappropriate for me to go. Although I would have gladly sacrificed my life for them, I feared that my presence would be misunderstood."

This was because one of the English gentleman's friends had adopted Sofia and he wasn't familiar with the friendship between the two families. Another reason which prevented him from going was that he was concerned about the religious and communal differences between them.

"Although I could not bear this, my friend, I was not crazy enough to meet her because in doing so I would have risked ruining her reputation, and you know, affairs like this one usually end badly."

Since he was concerned about his beloved's reputation he thought it better to quell the desires of his heart and his restlessness; this shows the equanimity of his disposition.

"God forbid she is harmed. The effects of love are far-reaching."

These thoughts had occupied his heart because of the social and religious differences between them and their changing circumstances.

"Really, what business does she have with me? When she is a stranger what intimacy would there be between us? What can one do if one is full of desire? Indeed, no one has the right to demand love. A lover might die from desire if he even glances at his beloved's shoes. What can one do about such dying?"

That was the era of Mirzā Ruswā's youth. Now the mood of love had changed altogether.

"Her condition is naturally obvious to me, and my thoughts for her well-being were entirely selfless."

It is possible that the change Mirzā Ruswā felt in her personality was an illusion, and she had not changed at all. Perhaps she would meet him now just as she had met him earlier. His perception of the relationship had changed. This reminds me of a verse by someone:

"What beauty youth has brought upon her, O heart! Why be chaste! Now we too should change our intentions!"

But Mirzā Ruswā remained patient and bore with the situation as we can see in this speech:

"There was never any flirtation in her conversation, nor any coquetry in her glances. Alas! O Ruswā! As a consequence of your love, you wander in her lanes. Why should she call you? What obligation does she have to converse with you? Why should she love a wanderer like you? Why should she be intimate with a madman like you? Who are you that she should give her heart to you or show compassion to you? Such was the situation for a long time. My life became miserable, I was overwhelmed with sadness. Sorrow had given rise to maddening thoughts, and all my wounds became unhealable sores. Restlessness began to destroy me. My love tested the limits of my patience."

But he never spoke of his condition to anybody, rather:

"I hid this secret from my heart itself because I was testing my ability to endure this pain. A war was waged between love and wisdom, and I was plagued by this battle day and night. I tried to restrain my desires, I tried to rid myself of this conundrum. It is better to burn in a fire than to burn day and night with the unfulfilled desires of one's heart."

But this love eventually bore fruit—nothing could prevent it from blossoming—

"The problems that come upon one cannot be shirked. The truth is that death cannot be shirked."

Unfortunately, after this, many pages of the *maśnavī Nālā-e Ruswā* have been lost. I only give below the incidents that are known from other sources.

By conjecture we know that after the death of Miss Sāhiba's mother and father, one of their close friends sent her to a hill-station and their property was possessed by the court.

At this time, God alone knows the extent of Mirzā Ruswā's suffering. We can just talk about these things: keening and wailing, suffering disgrace and being consumed by restlessness. He would stay awake all night, count stars, lie all day with his face covered. Hunger would disappear, his face would become pale, his lips dry. He would murmur strange things to his own heart. He hated social gatherings and preferred to wander in deserted places instead. He spent his time reading lovelorn verses, or writing them himself. But from these things one can hardly testify to the serious condition of someone's heart; the one who experiences this is the only one who knows. Love is such a terrible thing that even meeting the beloved is not enough. What can be said of the restlessness of separation! The truth is that—

"God should not put anyone in this situation."

The passion of love had overpowered Mirzā Ruswā from that very moment, but the blow that came afterwards almost killed him. But I will postpone telling you about that last blow, and tell you about some other terrible incidents that followed this one.

After the death of his uncle, his entire property was confiscated by his cousin. In his lifetime, his uncle wished that Ruswā would marry his daughter, who now owned the property. However, Ruswā had refused to marry her for some reason. Perhaps the reason was his love for Sofia, but we do not know this for sure. All that is known is that until his uncle's death, there was great amity between the cousins. But ever since his cousin was married, her adoration for Mirzā

Ruswā turned into hatred. For this reason, he began worrying about what would become of him after his uncle's death. Anyway, while his aunt was alive she considered him part of her family. After her death the biggest problem he faced was that he had no home. Although the house was to be inherited by his father, since his father had been banished he had no claim over the house. Even if he had been on good terms with his cousin he would not have tolerated living with her, and of course he could not be dependent on her goodwill now that their relationship was ruined. At this point, Gul-čehrā, one of his nurses, came to his rescue. He began living with her. He registered in a school and began learning English. He was very distressed in those days, but luckily he had recourse to divine support at this time. This tale is very amusing. I heard about it from one of his school friends.

In those poverty-stricken days, he was once studying in the classroom when the school master called for him and removed an envelope from his pocket. After confirming his name and his uncle's name he said, "Someone has sent one hundred rupees to you. Although the envelope and letter is addressed to me, the scribe did not write his name. Here is the letter."

Mirzā Ruswā took the cash, the envelope and the letter.

This divine occurrence did not happen only once but occurred frequently in his student days. However, since these letters came through the Sāhib, other people came to know about them.

He must have been studying in the school for about six or seven years when Miss Sāhiba's property was relinquished by the court and she came to live in her bungalow in Lucknow. But who knows what had happened to Ruswā because he never visited her. Mirzā Ruswā himself has composed verses about the conditions of that time which I provide here. I see that Mirzā Sāhib has worked very hard on these verses. He does not express his sentiments openly. He tries to hide them, but they don't remain hidden. There is a fine nuance in these verses which the audience will understand.

These thoughts are of the time when she had returned from the hill-station.

"There was this thought in my heart that I am poor and she is wealthy. She is of an unknown community, and of a different religion. I shall not visit her lest whatever relationship that remains may be ruined."

There is no doubt that Mirzā Ruswā is a man of honour, careful in his dealings and very cautious as well.

"There was a special relationship because of our elders, but now neither the people nor those circumstances exist anymore. How strange it is that that courtesy is no more, and that things are no longer the way they were. The heart has unattainable desires and it is not necessary for one to fulfil them. Whether or not the sadness of separation is terrible, whether or not the restless heart knows repose, it is appropriate now to contain the heart. It is necessary now to be patient."

Alas! He must have composed this verse with great passion.

"Poverty causes humiliation. If you love, keep it in your heart! What is this thought of union? Of what value is this heart? Leave these worthless thoughts aside. No one will ask after the condition of your heart. The circumstances must have changed, her nature must have changed. Gone are those days and those nights. There are no warm meetings any longer, lest there be any disgrace. If she does not meet me, it will merely add insult to injury. I accept that she has virtuous qualities, but I am a man and she is a woman. We claim equality, and I have taken pride in this notion of equality. But shyness is natural to the temperament of women. There is modesty in their disposition."

Two or three verses are worthy of our attention from here onwards.

"And then a few things happened, which made me embarrassed to talk to her. It became necessary for me not to visit her and to hide myself from her. I don't know why she bestowed her kind favour upon me. Why should I think that I felt love towards her and that it was not some sort of infatuation? She is well-mannered and intelligent too. Ah! She is my reward for some good deed that I must have done in the past. The world says that I should keep the embarrassing incidents of my life to my self, if I care at all about respect. Showing my face to her would be against my self-respect."

"Why boast of the sincerity of my intentions and the sacrifices I made? Of what use is nominal gratitude? The problem is that I expected a favour for the favour that I had done her. It is possible to expect a favour in return for a favour only when it is possible for the favour to be returned. However, when there is no possibility for the realization of the favour, then why should one expect a favour?"

Mirzā Sāhib's conjecture was obviously correct. So he writes:

"Ruswā! Let go of all those childhood memories, forget now that time and that age. In that age there was intimacy. I worry now whether that bygone love could be a reason for hatred. She may not like to be reminded of our intimacy, and those old rituals may have no hold on her anymore. What if she pretends not to recognize me and tries to hide her true feelings and feels bad about it?"

"Ruswā! Why these sighs and pleas? Why do you think she would still love you? For heaven's sake! Who are you? Why would someone fall in love with you? I was once her friend. O heart! Remind me if you remember that time. Why this melancholia, Ruswā? Why again this pointless wailing?"

Mirzā Ruswā sat silently contemplating these things. It was at this time that he received the following letter. I give below a word for word translation of the letter.

My dear friend—

Truly you are unconcerned about our friendship. I have been overwhelmed with trouble and you seem scarcely to have noticed. My mother and father both passed away. I was sent miles away from this city. It was as though I was imprisoned for many years. Surely you must have known these things, but sadly enough, you did not write me a single letter.

I did not know your address otherwise I would have written to you earlier. I discovered from my maidservant's daughter, whose husband works as a servant in Martinère College that you study there, so I have written to you at that address—surely you will receive this letter. Reply soon. Better still come here yourself. If you have any compassion, any ounce of loyalty, then come and see me. I still live in the same ancestral home where we played in our adolescence. Those trees which we climbed to disturb the birds in our childhood still stand there. That pool in which we splashed around for hours still stands there. The memory of that day when you were upset and sat under a date tree and

I was annoyed and sat in the cottage is still fresh in my mind.

Forget about those terrible matters of the past, in friendship there is no room for such trivial reservations. Do you not think that I am human? If that is so then I regret your mistrust and you should ask me for forgiveness. I ask for your forgiveness for writing these last few sentences. It's possible that you might have not come to see me for some other reason that I am not aware of. Anyway, come now and come soon. I have a favour to ask you, which would not be appropriate for me to mention in this letter.

Your friend from adolescence,
Sofia

The correct translation is the one I have written above, but I think that Mirzā Ruswā has transcribed this letter differently in *Nālā-e Ruswā*. There is not much difference between this translation and that one. However, one difference which is crucial is that Sofia has addressed him as "my dear friend" while Mirzā Ruswā inserts his *nom de plume*. By extrapolation we know that until that moment, Sofia did not know of his poetry or of his pen-name.

The letter is as follows: "Dear Ruswā, I haven't seen you for ages. A lot of troubles have befallen me, great disasters have befallen me. You didn't come even once to ask after me. I did not expect that from you. Was amity restricted only to our elders? Alas! What has happened to that cordiality? Oh how I remember those people and why wouldn't I remember them fondly? In fact they were the only good people I knew. My father loved you dearly, and my mum dearest was intimate with you as well. You used to visit them often, frolic and play with me all day. However, after their death you turned away from me. You seem to have abandoned all thought of me. You seem to have forgotten all the warmth and courtesy of our childhood days. Have you forgotten how to maintain a friendship? Do you not remember our childhood games? Do you not remember our adolescent meetings? That house and that garden have not been uprooted. That house and that garden are not too far away. If you came across that house and garden in your wandering, your feet would not tire from the excursion."

"How ungracious and discourteous you are! Heaven forefend the one who loves you! Ours is the inseparable union of two souls. Where does one find again the inseparable friendship that one had with a childhood friend? I didn't know the address of your house, nor did I know anything of your whereabouts. Ever since that ancestral house was dug up, I have become uncertain of any landmarks. I have been thinking of you since yesterday, and I have written this letter with a lot of difficulty. I hear that you are studying at Martinère. If that is true then this letter will not be lost. How strange if it does indeed reach you in a timely fashion? Do write back soon if you get this letter. Rather, what is the need for a response? Come yourself if you have time."

"I know the reason that you stay away, but that is a silly excuse to hide your face. If you are human then so am I. Do you think I am completely innocent? I understand that you are a man with self-respect, but I think that false pride is keeping you away. I know your heart is pure, so let's forgive our mistakes in friendship.

Waiting expectantly for the boundless joy that will come with your arrival,

Your candid friend,
Sofia"

Mirzā Ruswā has written about getting this letter in his *maśnavī Nālā-e Ruswā* with such enthusiasm that it is not possible to praise it enough. He has begun with the *sāqī-nāma*[9] which I give here:

"Ply me with water of life O saqi, so that I am freed from the anxiety of death. Death is the reason that my desires cannot be fulfilled because I'm scared that I may die of happiness if my desires are fulfilled. O saqi, give me medicine, so that my sadness and despair may disappear. For aeons I have suffered from an unhealable wound. Something should serve as a support for my life, so that the wounds in my heart can heal."

"You are the doctor for the ailment of separation; you are the medicine for the fever of love. But first listen to all my complaints, so that you may find a cure for them all. You are familiar with my disposition, and you know well the cure for my ailment. You have in your power a magnificent cure, which will allow health to return soon. Although that medicine is unique, the cure is in your hands. The thorn of grief pierces my heart, a kernel of pain lies in my heart. For aeons there has been an unhealable wound in my heart, and I have been preoccupied with maddening thoughts."

9 A poem in which the poet addresses Sāqī, the wine-bearer.

"I abhor medicine, water and food. I haven't eaten a morsel in ages. If I even think of eating I feel nauseous. There isn't a drop of blood in my body because I've slit my wrists and blood has drenched my sleeves. I am unable to sleep all night, I have a headache all the time. This is my state, having suffered sadness and every now and then pain washes over my heart. The strength of my body keeps on waning, while the onslaught of old-age continues strengthening. I keep waiting for death, and my bones are afflicted with fever."

This was his state earlier. After having received the letter, he was overwhelmed with happiness, which he describes as follows:

"Bring me musk scented wine, O saqi! I drink and you ply me with drink, O saqi!

Now I am unable to continue waiting, bring me a cup of wine. O fate! O fortune! Welcome! How lucky I am that I have finally been blessed by fortune! O sky! Congratulate me because I am freed from this prison of grief. A messenger of pleasure, an amulet for the heart—a letter from my gracious beloved appeared."

"Now there is only me and the house of my beloved. No trepidation on account of the gate-keeper who guarded you, nor any fear of enemies. Distress left the abode of my heart because my wishes were fulfilled. I received acknowledgement of my grief. I received all that my heart desired. The night is bewitched. It is the night of waiting for the night. Be happy my heart! For it is the day of Eid. Be happy my eye! That is the day of sight!"

Although that night passed with difficulty—yet:

"Making a thousand excuses to my heart I passed the night with great difficulty. At the crack of dawn, I refreshed myself and left the house. I walked determinedly to the house of my rosy-cheeked, adorable beloved. My darling met me congenially, and my heart was conquered by her conversation. First she complained of our separation, and then blamed me for my abhorrent behaviour. Ultimately, I became shame-faced and agreed that I was the one at fault."

"What could I tell her of the reasons that I had stayed away. I could say nothing except 'You are right.' My excuses weren't accepted, friends, and I couldn't tell her what was in my heart. It wasn't appropriate to tell her about my abject poverty. How could it have been appropriate to tell her this? How could I be exempted from blame? Since she was right, how could excuses have worked? The situation was a worrisome one. The problems were very difficult to resolve. When I took the blame on myself, she trusted that I loved her deeply. Then my faults were forgiven, and thus my problems were solved."

After that they started talking about important things—

"This remonstrance was necessary for the conversation that followed. 'If you promise to agree, I will say something. Otherwise what is the point? let me remain quiet."

"Then she began to say 'O Ruswā! I desire only one thing from you. All are concerned only about their own profit. The truth is that the world is a selfish place. I hope that my asking you for a favour is not futile. Why should I state it, if you will not agree to it? That's why I ask from you an avowal. For it is a task of great effort and a test of your affection for me.'"

"She won my heart with her conversation. She took my hand in hers and my word. Then the beautiful maiden parted her lips and started talking. 'The trouble is that I am of the female sex, and I worry about my environs day and night. I can't do this work, I cannot accomplish this task. This requires some effort—it requires your help.'"

"This job is not for me, and I can't trust a stranger with it either. Take this burden on your shoulders. Take on the role of my general agent. Take this power from me. Look through the documents with the details of employment, and make the necessary arrangements to ensure the safety of my environs, and quell those who are arrogant and make advances on me. Don't consider this as mere employment; rather, think of it more as your responsibility. You know my natural temperament and my disposition.'"

"Hearing the instructions of the beautiful one, I wanted to refuse her, but I couldn't on account of our friendship. In addition, my desire to meet her prevented me from doing so."

"Although it was against prudence, I could not refuse her outright. My misguided heart was telling me that I would accede to her for these reasons. My heart leaned towards her. It claimed her for its own. Love has nothing to do with prudence and is unconcerned with honour and reputation. Still I said in a soft voice, 'Do you think I am capable of doing this work? Tell me what I should do because I have neither experience nor wit. I am incapable of shrewd-management and I feel that I am unworthy of handling your affairs. Truly, I am not capable—you need a more experienced proctor. Although I will try my best, it is still possible that there might be some losses. I hope you understand what I am telling you, and that you are also taking other people's advice.'"

"Annoyed, she said—'what advice? What do you have to do with my happiness? I do not believe that there will be losses. My heart is content.' I said that it is probable that I would make mistakes, but she laughed and said she is fine with that."

"She said, 'Why do you ignore my request for no reason? Why do you find counterarguments in vain? Why are you giving me weak apologies? There is a limit to peevishness. No more excuses will work. No more evasions can be fashioned. I have explained the job to the best of my ability. Why don't you tell me clearly that you refuse it? Go away! I have seen the depth of your affection for me. Don't you dare say now that you love me. Think what you wish of me in your heart.

Think of me as a stranger or think badly of me. I didn't think you would be this unkind. By God I swear, you are short-sighted. You think my job will bring you disgrace. You think that I am not to be trusted.'"

"When that one who is as beautiful as the moon was upset, I was perturbed, and decided to make an excuse for my diffidence. I said, 'I am agreeable to this in every way. How could I refuse you? I will be diligent in every possible way, I promise you that with my heart and my soul, and you know I am a man of my word. What disgrace can there be in serving you? I am ashamed of my mistake in refusing you. In fact, I am honoured by the favour you have bestowed upon me, and I take great pride in my future. I consider it a token of your favour. I hope your heart understands what I mean. No one can ignore the great kindness inherent in this favour.'"

"She laughed and said, 'You have distanced yourself from me. I understand that you have tremendous pride. From today you must respect our friendship above all else, and forsaking me is against our friendship. You have been negligent, but you are forgiven.' In short, after many loving words between us, she became stubborn and had me pledge that

I would work for her. I started work the very next day and began making arrangements for her house."

In short, what happened is that the bequest came to be in Mirzā Ruswā's name. He stayed for a few days in Lucknow. He wrote down all that Miss Sāhiba could remember about her environs. When he went to her property he was faced with many troubles. According to some people, he had never seen a rice field. In truth, he was a creature of the city, of a refined temperament, unfamiliar with rustic ways, so for a few days the villagers took advantage of his naiveté. But if one is determined and is truly concerned about something, then one eventually finds a way. Mirzā Sāhib's servant Nawroze Alī was very familiar with the work of a farmer. Mirzā Sāhib called for him from Lucknow and put him in charge of the district. He made such fine arrangements that they laid all of Miss Sāhiba's fears to rest. Eventually, he too became familiar with the goings-on of the village. The work progressed and the situation remained ideal for many a year.

Mirzā Ruswā and Miss Sofia's relations were similar to those between an English man and his betrothed. Rings had been exchanged.

They had proclaimed their undying love for each other. In truth their relationship was more like that of lovers, in fact that of a married couple. Their intentions were pure. The fires of passion were aflame. Both were being consumed in the same fire. Both impatient. Both restless. A test of patience and of endurance. In short, they were in a strange state and only those who have experienced such a state can understand their condition.

It was at this time that Miss Sofia disclosed her intention of going to Bombay. She told Mirzā Ruswā, "Wait here, I will be back in seven or eight days," but Mirzā Ruswā could not bear to be away from Miss Sofia for so long, so he insisted on coming along and eventually she agreed. Both of them left happily for Bombay. On reaching there they rented two rooms in a hotel. Mirzā Ruswā lodged in one and Miss Sofia in the other. They travelled around Bombay quite a lot. They would leave by car in the morning and would roam the city until evening. When it was time for a meal they would go to a restaurant or take a picnic along with them. They would frequent theatres in the evenings. In short, for a week they had a merry time.

One day Miss Sāhiba began complaining early in the evening, "I have a headache, I won't go for the show this evening." She retired to her room at nine in the evening after her dinner. Mirzā Ruswā retired to his room as well. Every morning, the two of them would have tea together. The next day it was later than usual and there was still no sign of Miss Sāhiba. Mirzā Ruswā waited for an hour or so thinking "Perhaps she remained unwell last night, so she is probably still asleep." When some time had passed, he went anxiously to her door and knocked, but no one responded. In his heart Mirzā Ruswā exclaimed, "Oh God! What's the matter?" To enter into someone's bedroom without their permission is against English etiquette, but how long could he wait? He eventually opened the door. At first he called out to Miss Sofia, but when he got no response from her he strode in. Miss Sāhiba was nowhere to be seen, the room was empty. Mirzā Ruswā felt faint. He made inquiries with the hotel staff and found that Miss Sāhiba had asked for a car at eleven o'clock last night to go somewhere.

Mirzā Ruswā was utterly taken aback. He was perplexed about why she went and where she could have gone when his gaze fell on an envelope on the table on which his name was written in Miss Sāhiba's hand.

He quickly opened the envelope. The following was written:

My beloved,

Don't be saddened by my sudden disappearance of which I did not inform you. The truth is that I hadn't come to Bombay only for pleasure but for a special purpose. I didn't think it appropriate to tell you about it. I recently discovered in Lucknow that my aunt who lived in Paris left an inheritance of crores[10] when she passed away. I am the sole inheritor of her vast estate. From the letter of her general agent I understand that her will is in my name, but to claim my inheritance I need to go to Paris:

First, I need to understand the state of my finances and second there is a lot of land and real-estate there, which I need to sell.

I think of you as my husband and of Lucknow as my home and in truth it is so. But you do understand that it is necessary for me to go for this reason, don't you? And the reason I didn't take you along with me was because people abroad including most of my distant relatives might not have liked our relationship and that could create problems for me.

10 A monetary unit of measurement. One crore is equal to ten million.

In fact, it is possible then that I would not have had any success in settling matters. Most of the people over there, knowing that I am the inheritor of such a large estate will flatter me, so that they can gain my favour. I believe that the entire property, cash and goods included will be in my possession soon. I think I will be completely free in approximately three months. After all is accomplished, I won't remain there for a moment longer than necessary. In the meantime, I shall keep writing letters to you. There is no doubt that you consider me loyal, but just to ensure your peace of mind, I am putting all my property in Lucknow in your name. You will find the papers in my box.

When you get this letter I will have gone very far from Bombay. The ship named "Murweesberg" will leave for France at exactly twelve fifteen.

Please leave for Lucknow today and wait for three months. Then God will grant us the day when you and I will sit and enjoy music in the evening in our garden. You will be reading your *ghazals*[11] and I will be listening to them. Wait for a few more days.

Sincerely,
Your Sofia

11 A form of Urdu poetry which consists of several *shers* (composed of two half-line verses) which are independent in their meaning from each other but which have the same rhyme scheme.

Bombay—The Grand Hotel
18—

PS- Keep my garden in order. I am concerned about the geranium trees that I have planted. Keep an eye on the gardeners—they shouldn't abandon the garden.

On reading this letter Mirzā Ruswā's heart suffered much, but then he calmed his heart and left for Lucknow. One letter came from Aden. Two or three letters came from Paris, in which there were details of the legal proceedings. Then there was a telegram from Paris when [Sofia] was leaving that city.

"I am leaving on a ship called 'Utopia' for India today."

After receiving the telegram, Mirzā Ruswā began counting not only the days but also the minutes. Alas! That ship came neither that day nor the day after.

Mirzā Ruswā's friends think something else, but it would not be appropriate to write of it here. Those who can understand it, will.

Every morning and evening water is sprinkled in the garden. Each leaf of the trees is carefully washed. Chandeliers are lit in every corner. In the courtyard two chairs are laid out in the evening. Pots of geraniums surround the place that Mirzā Ruswā himself sits. A notebook of *ghazals* is kept before him. An organ is placed before a chair. His eyes are trained on the door. Even today he waits for his faithful beloved. Fifteen years have passed since that day, but his passion for her remains unchanged. He is fine the whole day, but in the evening he gets an attack of madness and is unable to stay himself. May God take pity on his condition.

Death will come one day saying this
Today she comes, tomorrow she comes

WORKS CITED

ASADUDDIN, M. "First Urdu Novel: Contesting Claims and Disclaimers." *Annual of Urdu Studies* 16.i (2001): 76-97. *Index Islamicus.* Web. 30 Sept. 2008.

RUSWĀ, Mirzā Muhammad Hādi. *Junūn-e Intezār Ya'nī Fasānā-e Mirzā Ruswā.* Lucknow, Awadh: Gulāb Singh Press, 1899.

A REVIEW

The Earliest Extant Review of
Umrāo Jān Adā

Taken as a whole, this take [*qiṣṣa*; i.e. *Umrāo Jān Adā*] is written on the same model that Mr. Reynolds[1] used to write *Rosa Lambert*.

1. George William MacArthur Reynolds (1814-1879) was one of the two Western writers most translated and popular in Urdu between the 1890s and the 1920s, the other being Marie Corelli (1855-1924). At least three of the latter's novels were translated into Urdu by Ruswā, but none of the former's. (At least none has so far been identified). For an incomplete listing of such translations, see Mirzā Ḥāmid Bēg, *Maghrib sē Naṣrī Tarājim* (Islamabad: Muqtarida Qaumī Zabān, 1988). (The book is still quite useful despite its innumerable errors of editing and printing. Bēg lists five separate translations of Rosa Lambert, all published at Lucknow.) Ruswā's translations of cheap potboilers have long been out of print, but at least one was edited and published more recently; Mirzā Muḥammad Hadī Ruswā, *Khūnī 'Ishq*, Ed. Muḥammad Maẓāhiru 'l-Ḥaq. Patna: Educational Society, 1987. It is a translation of Corelli's play, *Wormwood: A Drama of Paris*.

The difference is this: Rosa Lambert has herself told everyone her life story and her shameless indiscretions (*sharmnāk bēbākiyāṅ*), whereas in the case of this novel neither has *Umrāo Jān "Adā"* written it nor does it contain such shameless indiscretions as would make it unfit to be read before one's female family members [*bahū bēṭiyōṅ*]. [Umrāo Jān] told it all to her confidant (whose name is Mirzā Ruswā Sāhib), and he had it published. Further, the former (i.e. Rosa Lambert) is an imagined story, while the latter, according to Mirzā Ruswā Sāhib, is factual. Rosa Lambert disgraced herself out of spite; Umrāo Jān could not remain chaste due to matters beyond her control. Similarity in its [many] incidents distracts the reader's attention from Rosa Lambert, but [*Umrāo Jān Adā*], besides being not repetitious in its events, is in fact extremely interesting—in particular because of its frequent interludes of refined humour. Thought-provoking verses, delightful natural scenes, colourful private assemblies for dance and music, vividly described public entertainments and fairs, narratives of sufferings [at home] and travails in exile, tales of treachery and deception, accounts of true love, stories of the sagacity as well as foolishness of the rich and the noble—[they can all be found in this book].

Since Umrāo Jān was a courtesan [*tawāif*] and a well-versed musician, we are also treated with frequent insightful remarks on the finer points of music. Equally displayed is a knowledge of physiognomy [*qiyāfa-shināsī*]. Most importantly, [the author] has sought to prove that the goodness or badness of a man's nature is not enough to make him good or bad; it is necessary that there should also be appropriate and conducive circumstances [*vāqi'āt*]. It has also been shown that a prostitute [*randī*] does not get a chance to improve her lot in the hereafter unless she possesses some innate ability or she is ugly looking, or she has grown old, or she has suffered some great misfortune. The reason for it is that there are always numerous people [around her] who would prize her lack of chastity and who would look with approval at her bold and shameless acts. It is these faults [of the prostitutes] that people count as their virtues. The delightfulness of the narrative and the excellence of the language can be gauged by the book's readers on their own. Price (illustrated): One rupee and twelve annas; (unillustrated): one rupee and eight annas.[2]

Junūn-e Intezār Ya'nī Fasānā-e Mirzā Ruswā

Bī Umrāo Jān, on seeing her own biography being published, has written all the intimate details of Mirzā Ruswā Sāhib's own life—in other words, she has vented her fury. But it too is not without its pleasure. It is also an example of Umrāo Jān's own talents.

Price: Three and one/half annas.

(*Me'yār*,[3] Lucknow, no 8, 1899)

2. It is intriguing that the first edition had two versions and that one, more costly, was 'illustrated [*bā-taṣvīr*]. No copy seems to have survived. It may be mentioned that at the time an edition that had a photograph on its cover (printed on glossy paper) was often considered "illustrated." There is also a legend that there was in fact a courtesan commonly known as "Kālī Umrāo" [Black Umrāo] and it was her picture that adorned the cover of the first edition.

3. The first reaction in Lucknow to the prevalent "decadent" poetry of Vazīr, Rind, Amīr, Dāgh and Jalāl was in the pages of *Avadh Panč*. This reaction was welcomed by most masters of poetry in that city. A prominent member of that group, Saiyyid 'Alī Naqī "Ṣafī," organized a literary society by the name of Dā'ira Adabiya, among whose members were such luminaries as Munshī Sajjād Ḥusain (the first editor of *Avadh Panč*), Mirzā Muḥammad Hadī "Ruswā," Shaikh Mumtāz Ḥusain 'Uṣmānī (the second editor of *Avadh Panč*) and Piyārē Ṣāḥib "Rashīd" (a famous elegy-writer). The gatherings of this society appear to have been literary salons where members

discussed literary and linguistic issues and collectively declared what was "acccptable" and "correct" in Urdu poetry. "Ṣafī" also established another literary society called Anjuman-e Me'yār-e Adab; it organized a monthly mushā'ira, hosted by different, more affluent members. These mushā'iras were ṭarḥī, and in the early years, the ṭarḥ was always chosen from some ḡhazal of Ghālib. The new ḡhazal were then published in a monthly anthology entitled Me'yār, which eventually became a monthly magazine, with additional literary matter, including infrequent reviews. [The preceding is based on the comments of Mirzā Ja'far Ḥusain on the mushā'iras of Lucknow in his informative book, Qadīm Lakhnau kī Ākhrī Bahār (New Delhi, Bureau for the Promotion of Urdu, 1981. Pp. 262-7).]

I happen to possess a bound volume of Me'yār for the year 1911. The average issue runs to 32 pages. The cover is printed in black on green, with an elaborate design. Within the frame of a vine there is a map of India with "Hindustān" visibly written in the Bay of Bengal, and "India" in the Himalayas. At the top there are dark rolling clouds through which two celestial shapes emerge: to the left, a crescent and star, with "Ghālib" inscribed in the crescent, and to the right, a big radiant sun, similarly inscribed "Mīr." A large standard on the left side of the page carries a flared banner, with the name of the magazine in large calligraphy and another crescent and moon above the name. The title also carries three separate Urdu inscriptions. (1) In a medallion on the left: "What could be a greater honor and greater good fortune for this journal than to perform its duties under the patronage of Urdu's foremost champion and the nation's most popular and influential well-wisher, the Honorable Ḥāmid 'Alī Khān Ṣāḥib 'Ḥāmid.' Barrister at Law." (2) Over and below the medallion is a verse: bāzār-e ḥusn mēṅ čal yūsuf kā sāmnā kar / khōṭē kharē kā parda khul jā'ēgā čalan mēṅ. "Come with me to the Market of Beauty and stand before Joseph: the buyers will soon make clear whose beauty is true and whose is false." (3) Down the left side runs another inscription: "Urdu literature's most authoritative critic and the most

powerful instructor of good taste. Edited by Ḥakīm
Sayyid ʿAlī Muḥsin Khān ʿAbr.' Printed at Meʿyār Press,
Čīnī Bāzār, Lucknow. Published at the Offices of Meʿyār."
Inside, "Abr" describes himself as a "Follower of Mīr
and Ghālib" and as the owner of the journal. Some of the
issues also carry a photograph of some poet or patron
of the journal, together with an account of his life and
work.

Each issue is in the main devoted to the ghazals written
for the monthly mushāʿira mentioned above. By this
time the tarh is rarely a line from Ghālib. The ghazals are
organized in two groups. The first consists of ghazals
specifically offered for inclusion in the monthly
"competitive" or "comparative" [taqābulī] section. But
the ghazals are not printed as separate entities. Instead,
couplets from the various submitted ghazals are
arranged together under the heading of the qāfiya that
they share. Another condition observed is that the
maṭlaʿ of each submitted ghazal contains the qāfiya of the
tarh in the second line. Further, the selected verses are
arranged by the alphabetical order of the poets' names
and not with regard to any distinction of seniority. The
second group contains other tarhi ghazals, presented
in the conventional manner, with all due regard to the
poet's seniority. Additionally, there are often brief
literary and philosophical essays as well as more poetry
in other genres.

Apparently the journal was printed on two kinds of
paper; the annual subscription for the better quality was
Rs 3; the lower quality cost a rupee less. Patrons paid Rs
12; Supporters, Rs 6; while the dues from rājas and
navābs [vāliyān-e mulk] were left to their magnanimity
[ʿālī-himmatī]. Of our further interest are the nine
"Principles and Duties" [uṣūl va farāʾiẓ] that the journal
listed on its inside back cover and which apparently
guided its contents. These are as follows:

1. To seek to develop Urdu literature in interesting
   and serious ways.

2. To display in practice what "Good Taste" [maẕāq-e
   salīm] is, so that there may come about a general
   desire to perfect one's abilities.

3. To nurture Urdu language and to follow "Good Taste."
4. To remove errors of craftsmanship and understanding.
5. To exclude in a good manner all ignoble themes.
6. To publish frequently useful essays on poetry and prose.
7. To be bold and independent, but with due civility, in proclaiming what is right.
8. To judge what is false and what is true, without any partisanship or prejudice.
9. To withdraw and abstain from religious debates and political arguments.

This review first appeared in the *Annual of Urdu Studies* (AUS) 15: 2000: 287-292. The publishers and editors are grateful to Professors Muhammad Umar Memon and C.M. Naim for permission to reproduce it here.

THE END

۲۴

مجھے امیدہوجم سے خوشامدین کام کرینگے۔یقین ہے کہ میتہ جلدکل جا ئگادا نقذار
جش میرے فتصد میں آ ئگا۔ میرے اندازے سے تین مامین مامین الکل فرصت
ہوجائگی۔اورچکہ ہد میں دم پہروبان نہ پہروں گی۔اِں ورمیان میں تم کو خطلہ
لکھتیاررہوگی۔اسمیں شک نہیں کہ جم مجھے وفادار جانتے ہو کہ مزید الطمینان
کے لئے میں نے گھڑی کی کل ہاداد کا بیج نام تمہارے نام کردیلے۔کا فذات
فرورئ میرے کبس مین موجودکین۔

مسرت تنگرہ خطلہ کا اپناپتی سے بہت درکل گئ ہوں گی۔جہاز گا مروتیں بگ
نامے ٹیک سہارا پارو بیک رواندہ ہوگا۔جس پہ میں فرانس جاتی ہوتا۔
تم آتا ہی اکسپوچلے جاؤ۔اورتین تیپیہ انظار کرو۔پھر خداوندکے کاکہ جم تم
ودلون بانغ کے کسمین شام کے وقت بیتچے ہوں گے۔مینا پہ باہرکہ تم اپنو۔لین
پہچتے ہوسکے میں سکی ہوں گی۔جندروز اور انظار کرو نقط

راقم
تمہاری مومنہ

بلی گرشتہ بوتل
ستمبر

کمربیتے
میرے باغ کو درست رکھنا چرانم کے ورخت جومین کے ورخت میں نے مشت لگا سے میں دھکا لچپے
بہت خیال ہے الی پر تاکید رکھا۔ جا نچ دھراپتں۔

اس خطلہ وکلام مرزارسیاکے دل پہ جوکچھ مدسہ گذرا گذرا گم پھر بول کوتسکین دیکے
کینوپچلے اٹے۔
ایک خطمدین سے اپناپتا۔دوتین خطمیرس سے آتے تھے۔اوثین مقدمات
کامفصل حال رہا۔اسکے بعد پرسم سے بداگا پو تھدتت ایک تا روبا۔
"جم آمگلا گوبیہ نامے جہازپہ ہندوستانی روانہ ہوتنے تہ
۱تارکے آنے کے ہدورن کیسے مرزارسیاکر ایں تکتے گے۔کمرہ جہازہ آمگلا آتامے
بکل۔

جایا کرتے تھے۔ آج معمول سے زیادہ دیر ہو گئی مس صاحبہ برآمد ہوئیں۔ گھنٹہ ڈیڑھ گھنٹہ مرزا رسوا نے انتظار کیا اس خیال سے کہ شاید رات کو مزاج درست نہ تھا۔ صبح کو آنکھ لگ گئی ہوگی۔ جب بہت دیر ہوئی تو کمرے کے دروازے پر جا کے دروازہ کو کھٹکایا کوئی آواز نہ آئی۔ مرزا رسوا دل میں کہتے ہیں یا اللہ کیا ماجرا ہے۔ سونے کے کمرے میں بلا اجازت چلے جانا انگریزی تہذیب کے خلاف ہے۔ مگر کہاں تک انتظار کیا جاتا آخر دروازہ کھولا۔ پہلے آواز دی جب جواب نہ آیا اندر گئے۔ دیکھا مس صاحبہ ندارد ہیں۔ کمرہ خالی پڑا ہے۔ مرزا رسوا کی آنکھوں میں اندھیرا سا آگیا۔ ہوٹل کے نوکروں سے پوچھا۔ معلوم ہوا مس صاحبہ نے رات کو گیارہ بجے گاڑی مانگی تھی سوار ہو کے کہیں گئیں۔

اب تو مرزا رسوا صاحب کے ہاتھ کے طوطے اڑ گئے۔ کیوں گئیں کہاں گئیں اسی شش و پنج میں تھے کہ لکھنے کی میز پر ایک لفافہ مس صاحبہ کے ہاتھ کا لکھا ہوا انکے نام کا ملا۔

جلدی جلدی لفافہ کھولا۔ لکھا تھا۔

میرے پیارے۔ تم میرے دفعتہً بے اطلاع غائب ہو جانے سے ملول نہ ہونا۔ بات یہ ہے کہ بمبئی میں صرف سیر و سیاحت کے لئے نہیں آئی تھی ایک خاص مطلب تھا۔ مگر اوسکا اظہار تم سے مناسب نہ تھا۔ مجھے لکھنؤ میں معلوم ہوا تھا کہ میری پھوپھی جو پیرس میں رہتی تھیں کروروں کی جائداد چھوڑ کے انتقال کر گئیں۔ سوا میرے اونکا کوئی وارث نہیں ہے۔ اونکے مختار کے خط سے معلوم ہوا کہ وصیت نامہ بھی میرے نام کا کر گئی ہیں۔ مگر اسکے لیے مجھکو پیرس جانا ضرور ہے۔

ایک تو حساب فہمی کے لیئے دوسرے اس مطلب سے کہ وہاں اکثر اراضی اور مکانات وغیرہ ہیں اونکو فروخت کرنا اور روپیہ نقد کر لینا ہے۔

میں تمہیں اپنا شوہر اور لکھنؤ کو اپنا وطن سمجھتی ہوں اور در حقیقت ایسا ہی ہے مگر اس معاملہ کے لیئے (تم سمجھ سکتے ہو) کہ میرا جانا ضروری تھا۔ اور تمکو ساتھ لیجانے میں یہ مصلحت تھی کہ ولایت کے لوگ جنمیں اکثر میرے دور کے رشتہ کے عزیز بھی ہیں تمہیں ہمراہ دیکھکر برا مانتے اور شاید میرے معاملات میں کچھ مشکلیں پڑ جائیں بلکہ ممکن تھا کہ ناکامیابی ہوتی۔ وہاں کے اکثر لوگ مجھے اتنی بڑی جائداد کی وارث

خلاصہ تقریر یہ ہے کہ مرزار سوا کے نام خط ارسا نامہ ہو گیا۔ چند روز لکھنو میں رہے طلاق کے حالات سے جہاں تک اس صاحب واقف ہیں اسی یاد و اختیں کہیں پھر علاقہ ہمہ گئے بیان انگریزی دونین پیش آیں بقول مجمع خط کا یہ بیت تک ندی کہتا ہے۔ اول تو یہ بہ لکھنو کے رہنے والے نازک مزاج آدمی بتکہ پودہ کاری کا یہ مسائل کہ چند روز گزارہ ون نے خوب بنایا۔ گر دل میں جس بات کا ارادہ و شوق ہوتا ہے اس کی کوئی نہ کوئی راہ نکل ہی آتی ہے۔ مرزا صاحب کا وکر نوروز علی کمائی کے کام میں بہت ہوشیار تھا کلکتہ سے اسے بلوا کے ضلع دار مقرر کیا واقعی قرار واقعی بند و بست کیا دفتر فہرہ وغیرہ واقف کار ہوتے کام چلنے لگا۔ کوئی سال تکلیف حال رہا۔

مرزار سوا اور مس سو فیہ کے تعلقات ویسے ہی تھے جو انگریزی منگیتر ون کا سنا ہتا ہے۔ انگوٹھیاں بدل گئی تھیں۔ جاوا اور بیاہ کے اقرار ہو چکے تھے۔ ظاہری بن بالکل انداز عاشقی معشوقی بلکہ میاں بیوی کا تھا۔ دلوں میں پاکیزہ قسم آتش شوق کے شعلے بلند تھے۔ دونوں ایک ہی آگ میں جل رہے تھے۔ دونوں بیتاب، دونوں بے قرار۔ مگر کا امتحان ضبط کی آزمائش۔ غرض کہ غضب حالات تھے جنکو گھر دیتی لوگ بھی سکتے میں نہیں ایسا عالم ہو۔

اس اثنا میں مس صاحبہ نے بمبئی جانے کا ارادہ ظاہر کیا۔ مرزار سوا صاحب سے کہا تم بین شہر و ین آخر سات دن میں چلی آدن گی گر اثیں تاب کیاں بھی سامنے چلنے کے لئے ضدک آخر النین بھی بھرا لیا۔ دونوں خوشی خوشی بمبئی روانہ ہوئے۔ بمبئی جا کے ہوٹل کے دو کمرے کرا کے بسم لیئے۔ ایک میں مرزار سوا کا و تازہ ہر میں خود آترین بمبئی کی خوب سیر سیر ہوئیں۔ صبح سے شام گاڑی بروسوا ہوکے کلا شام تک گشت کرتا۔ جب کھانے کا وقت آیا کسی ہوٹل میں اور تربے کہا نا کہا ایا الماری پر سامنے لے لیا۔ راون کو تھیرہ و بھی بمبئی جا تا۔ غرض کہ ایک ہفتے تک خوب تجسین کیا۔

ایک دن سر شام مس صاحبہ نے کہا میرے سینہ میں درد ہو آج میں تماشہ میں نہ جاؤن گی۔ کھانے والے سے فراغت کرکے نیچے سونے کے گری ہیں چلی گئیں۔ مرزار سوا بھی اپنی جگہ سو رہے۔ دوسرے دن صبح کیو وقت دونوں ایک سی ساتھ

٣١

گوبیں کو کشش کرون گا تا امکان
جو میں چشتا ہوں اور سکر سمجھو تو
یوٹی جنبلا کے مصلحت کیسی
جبکہ یاور نہیں کہ جو نقصان
عوض کی میں نے مجھے ہوتگے قصور
بات کو میری ٹالتے ہو عبث
عذر باطل پکس قدر کہ ہے
اسیں کچھ عذر دل نہیں سکتا
جیسے بھاچلی میں تیامقدم
دیکھیں گی میں نے آپ کی الفت
سب چھے دل میں آپ کو کیا سمجھے
تو کو فساد ہ جانتے تھے ہم
اگر ی میری جار مجھے ہو
جب بگڑنے لگی وہ ماہ لقا
کہ مجھے ہر طرح سے ہے منظور
تن دہی میں کرون گا سامان
مارکا ذکر کیا میں خاوم ہوں
بلکہ نازان ہوں اس عنایت پر
میں بانی کا ہ ہا سمجھا
اس عنایتیں جو نزاکت ہے
بنکمبولی بہت ہی دور ہو تم
آج سے ایک کام کیے گا
سمجھ ہر وہ دوستی کے خلاف
الغرض بعد محبت بسیار
پیری ی ممکن ہے ہو کو ٹا لقصان
اور لوگوں کی مصلحت ہے لو
آپ کو اس سے کیا ہماری خوشی
کچھ تو ہے میرے دل کو اطمینان
ہنس کے کہنے لگی نہیں منظور
مجھ میں کیوں نکالتے ہو عبث
کج ادائی کی بھی کوئی حد ہے
کوئی پہلو نکل نہیں سکتا
صاف کہدو و میں نہیں منظور
اب نہ کہنا کہ مجھ کو بھی الفت
غیر مجھ سے برا مجھے
کیسے بیبید مو خدا کی قسم
مجھ کو ہے اعتبار مجھے ہو
منفعل ہو کے میں نے عذر کیا
کرو نہ انکار سرا کیا مقدور
دل و جان سے ہوں بندۂ قرباں
خود ہی اپنی خطا پہ نادم ہوں
فکر ہے مجھ کو اپنی قسمت پر
دل میں تر خود سمجھ لو کیا سمجھا
اس کو مجھ پہ کس طاقت ہے
ماتی ہوں بٹھے گیو رہو تم
دوستی کو سلام کیے گا
آپ بھی میں پھر قصور معاف
اس نے ضد کر کے لیا اقرار

دو سبے دون سے کام کرنے لگا
گر حسب انتظام کرنے لگا

پڑ دیکھے گی کہ اسے رسوا
نفع ذاتی ہے ہے نظر سب کی
میر اکہنا کہیں منقول نہ ہو
ایسے قصے لیتی ہوں اقرار
دائمی ہے وہ کام محنت کا
باتوں باتوں میں دل سے سوچ لیا
بہرہ ہے درفشانِ طلب گفتار
بات سے پرکھتی ہوں حریتِ ذات
مجھے یہ کام ہو نہیں سکتا ہے
اسمیں کچھ جدوکد کی حاجت پر
میرے لائق یہ کاروبار نہیں
اپنے ذریعہ کام تجھ سے
ہوکے میری طرف سے قلم عذار
خود علاقہ کا بند و بست کرو
ڈگری کا نہ سلسلہ سمجھو
تم چاہتے ہو میری خصلت کو
سنتے اور یہ قصہ کی پچ گفتار
دوستی کے خیال سے رہ کا
گوکہ قضا میری مصلحت کے خلاف
کہہ رہا قضا اور میرا دل گراہ
دل طرف خدا ہو گیا اور سب کا
عشق کو مصلحت سے کام نہیں
ہری بری میں نے دلی زبان سے کہا
پیکے گیا اسمیں دخل ہے مجھکو
میں کہاں حسن انتظام کہاں
راضی میں نہیں ہوں ہون وقت کار

تم سے اک مدعا بھی ہے میرا
پیسے دنیا چاہنے مطلب کی
کیوں کہوں میں اگر قبول نہ ہو
کہیں الیاسا نہ ہو کہ ہو انکار
امتحان ہے تمہاری الفت کا
ہاں نہیں ہاتھ دے سے کے قول لیا
اسطرح ورحذر ہوئی وہ نگار
اور علاقہ کی فکر ہے دن رات
کچھ مرا انجام ہو نہیں سکتا ہے
کچھ تمہاری مدد کی حاجت ہے
جیسے کا مجھکو اعتبار نہیں ہے
اختیارات عام لو مجھ سے
جاینے لو کا خذات اسای دار
جو کہ سرکش میں اونکو بست کرو
اسکو اپنا اسا لمہ سمجھو
جانتے ہو مری طبیعت کو
چاہتا ہوں کہ میں کرو نہ انکار
آرزو سے وصال سے وہ کا
گر ایچھا نہ قضا جواب صاف
یا بنابی پوچھ سے گا خدا مخواہ
دی یا ہر ہو گیا اور سب کا
اسکو یہ واسطے ننگ و نام نہیں
چل سکے گا یہ کام مجھ سے کیا
تجھ ہے ہے دخل ہے مجھکو
میں کہاں اور اہتمام کہاں
پجر یہ کار ہا ہے ہیے مختار

اب بہیں ثاب انظار بھے   میرے دے ہمام خوشگوار ہے

مرحبا یا نفیس یا ثمت   را وہ آکتم تو شاثمت

آسان لجھکو دے سدیار کیا و   کہ جوا قدہ غم سے میں آزاد

قاصد شوق مرزہ جان لایا   تا سہ یار بہسہ بان آیا

یہ بہر ن اب اور کستان حبیب   یہ غم یا سباں دخوف رقیب

غاند دلی سے کہنتین خلین   حسود لخزا و حسرتین خلین

لکئی فسم کی داو نتہ ماٹھی   یا لی دل کی مراد تمنہ کا ملی

اہ گو یا کہ بے برات کی رات   اور بے انظار رات کی رات

مژدہ دل کے عیداد ن ہے   مژدہ اے چشم دیدکا دن ہے

خوشک وہ رات بھاڑ ہوگی۔ گر

دل سے میلے ہزار باک رے   رات کاٹی خدا اندا کر کے

صبح جوتے ہی اپنے بستر سے   بانہ تمہد د ہو کے ہم جلے گھر سے

ماز م کوئے گلعذار جبینے   جاکے اوس شنوع سے دو چار بوے

دوستاد لی وہ جان جہان   اوسکی بات نے دل ہوا قربان

پلے شکوے ہوے جدائی کے   فکر بہر میری کی ادائی کے

بکو جونا قاصد سارا آخر   میں جبرے کہا ہمگار آخر

کیوں نہ آنے سیا وعدہ کیا کتے   ثرہ بتا تھم بچہ سمجا کتے

عذر یا رہ ہان مشتا ذکیا   دل میں جو تھا بیان کیا نہ گیا

ذکر افلاس تا مناسب تھا   اونے کتے یہ کیا مناسب تھا

سرے الزام کس طرح لمتا   وہی بچے نے عذر کیا چلتا

بات میں بچکے کتے اولجا دے   سخت مشکل نے جک سلہادے

حبیب کتا ہ اپنا ہم نے مان لیا   جان ثار اودنے اپنا جان لیا

پر خطا میں جری سمات ہوئین   گفتیاں جو ثریکا تہین تھا ہوئین

اکلیدہ طلب کی باتیں شرماوی ہوئین۔

بتقاوادی وجدسے یہ گفتن وشنید   اوسی مطلب کی بنی یہ سب نبید

قول ہارد آکمہ زباں کہین   ورہ کیا خانہ وہ چپ ہی رہین

نظر لطف بے نہایت کی
آپ کی دو دست بے ریا سو فیام

اس خط کے آنے کا مآل مرزا نے اپنی مثنوی نالۂ رسوا میں جس جوش سے
سلاست تحریر کیا ہے وہ اتنی اور سلی قرینے نہیں ہوسکتی ۔ ابتدا ایک مآئی نامہ سے
کی ہے جسکو ہم عینہ نقل کئے دیتے ہیں ؎

جی کو ساقی بلا سے عذاب حیات
بسکہ ہے وجہ نا مرادی مرگ
وہ داد سے کریں فکر ہو دور
ہوں کم آثار میرے سینے کے
طلب میری لطیفی فرقت ہے
پہلے حسن میں خسائیں کیا کیا
تا ہے میرے سراپا سے واقت
قطرے قطرے میں بے عجب اکسیر
کوئی ناباب و دو داوّلی ہے
خاطر کی کشاکش پیوند دل میں
ہر تن سے بگڑ میں ہے ناسور
جی کو بالکل دو داسے لذت ہے
ہر تن سے غذا نہیں کھسائی
قطرۂ خون نہیں جیر تن میں
نیندآتی نہیں چھوٹے شب بھر
رہ بہ حالت بے پئی سے بہ کے
گھستی جاتی ہے جسم کی طاقت
موت کا انتظار رہتا ہے

با کہ شورش موت سے ہو نکات
خون یہ جگہ دوں زخادی مرگ
دو تن سے جگر میں ہے ناسور
دغم بھر جائیں میرے سینے کے
تو دوائے تپ محبت ہے
ایک ہی ساتھ ہر دو سب کی دوا
بہر غرض کے علاج سے واقت
جس سے محبت میں کچھ ہو نافیر
لگر تربیت حیات میں رضا بھی ہے
درد کی کچھ کسک پیارے دل میں
دو تن سے دل غم میں پڑ جاتا ہے
بلکہ اب سوفذا سے نفرت ہے
نامے بن دوڑ آئے او بکا نی
پہلے جو غذا وہ آب پڑے دامن میں
درد رہتا ہو سر میں آکٹھ پہر
چوکیا گشتی پہ دل میں زور کے
بڑھتی جاتی ہو ضعف کی شدت
پڑیوں میں بخا رہتا ہے

یہ تحریر کا مآل ہے خط آنے کے بعد جو خوشی اور سکا اظہار اس سطح کیا گیا ہے ؎
یادو شکبار لاسائی   میں چھوں اور تو ہا سائی

کہا ہو، اور مرزا رسوا اپنے تخلص کو داخل کرتے ہیں۔ قرینے سے معلوم ہوتا
ہے کہ سوفیہ کو اپنی شاعری اور تخلص سے اس وقت تک اطلاع دی جاتی۔

خطوں کو تم نے بھی پڑھا رسوا
ہم پر کیا کیا مصیبتیں گذریں
تم نے الگ خبر لے لی آ کے
کیا ہم دردوں پہ کچھ گذار کیا
یاد کرکے نہ آئیں اگلے لوگ
ہم بھلا کو کیا محبت کی
سامنے اکے آتے تھے اکثر
اوٹکھ مرتے ہی تھے مگر میرا
جو مسب رہے وہ اہل بھول گئے
کیا دیکھیں کے کس طرح یاد نہیں
اجی اور جائیں وہ گھر وہ باغ
چلے جہرتے اگر نکل آتے
کہتے تم کبھی ہے سرو ستہ ہو
عرق تساتقہ جڑ لی داسن کا
جھلک کر گھر کا پتا نہ کیا معلوم
کہ کیا سبب سے وہ قدیم کان
تم بہت یاد آتے ہو کل سے
مستقی ہوں ہاں نشتر میں ہو تم
کیا عجب دیکھ کر تیرے پہلو پہ
بلکہ کیا ہے جواب کی حاجت
جاتی ہوں جب سبب نکلے گا
تم جو انسان آمیں پی پڑے انسان
میں سمجھتی ہوں ہاں ان غیور ہو تم
خیرہ ہے کہ دل سے ہو تم صاف

مدتوں سے بھی نہیں دیکھا
کیسی کیسی قیامتیں گذریں
یہ وقت بھی شربتی تم سے
کیا ہو لی ے دہ کشادی
فی الحقیقت وہی تھا اچھا لوگ
اور میرگوئی قصہ الفت کئی
کیلئے کو دتے تھے وہ ون بھر
اہیں طرح کا خیال ہی چیھڑا
دوستی کا ناہ بھول گئے
وہ لڑکپن کے میل یاد نہیں
ذور آنکھیں وہ گھر دو باغ
اب کے وادن کمر نہ تک جاتہ
نہ اہمے کے سیگر الفت ہو
کہیں ملتا ہے دوست کہیں کا
تم کہاں جو ذرا اہے نہ معلوم
نہیں معلوم جھلک کھیک نشان
خط کہا ہے ہے جہنے اجمل سے
جو ہی چھے ہو خط ہو کہ تم
جلد لکشا جواب اگر ہو نے کا
خود ہی اڈ اگر لے فرصت
لئو ہے عذر منہ چھپانے کا
کیا سمجھے ہو مجھ کو تم ناد ان
رکھ سکجے بل میں اپنے گور ہو تم
دوستادہ شکایتیں ہوں ہن سعادت

وزارسوں صاحب۔ اِن خیالات سے خاموش ہوکے بیٹھ رہے تھے۔ گرم اوسی
دماغ میں یہ خط آکھڑا۔ جس کا ترجمہ لفظ بلفظ یہاں لکھا جاتا ہے
تیرہ جہاں سے دوست۔ واقعی تم نے بے عزت بڑھا دی ہم کو کیا کیا انگریز گزر
گئیں اور نئے خبر نہ لی۔ ان باپ بیٹوں نے تباہ کر کے ہم شہر سے کاٹے کوسوں
دور بیچ دیے گئے میرے سوں گیا تہہ دی جاسکے۔ تم کو ان باتوں کی خبر ضرور ہو دی
ہوگی۔ گر افسوس سہ سکتے تھا کہ یہ جو خط بھی کبھی نہ لکھا۔
مجھ کو تہہ آرا پتہ معلوم نہ تھا مگر میری طرف سے سہل ہو دی۔ اب آیا اِک کل کی
سے جس کا میاں دلبیر کالج میں اترکے رہے معلوم ہوا کہ تم دہاں پڑھتے ہوا وسی
بچ سے تم نے خط لکھا ہے یقین سے کہہ ضرور سے۔ جلد جواب دکھو۔ بلکہ خود آؤ۔
اگر تم میں کبھی نفاست اور وفاداری کا شائبہ ہو تو تم سے ضرور یہ وہ اُسی قدیم
کوئی میں آئے ہیں ۔ جہاں ہم لوگ کے دن میں کھیلا کرتے تھے۔ وہ وقت اب
تک موجود میں جب پیپر کے پیڑ بچوں کے گھونسلے اڑالا کرتے تھے۔ وہ حوض
اب بھی باقی ہے جس میں کشتیوں بھاپ سے چھپا یادی تھی وہ تمہارا اِک دل دروغ
جاتا اور گجر وکے درخت کے نیچے بیل کے نیچے جاتا اور رہ رہ آگر کے کوئی میں جلا
جانا آج تک آنکھوں میں پھرتا ہے۔
بعض امور کا جو تم نہیں خیال ہے اوسکو دل سے دور کرو۔ دوستی میں ایسی نازک
خیالوں سے کام نہیں جلتا۔ کیا تم جھ کو انسان نہیں سمجھتے اگر ایسا ہو تو مجھے
تمہاری بدگمانی پر افسوس ہے اور تہیں مجھ سے معافی مانگنا چاہیے۔ کم
میں تم سے خود معافی مانگتی ہوں کہ میں نے یہ دو دن کہہ کیوں لکھو کیوں ممکن
ہے کہ کسی اور وجہ سے نہ آ سکے ہو۔ بہر طور آؤ اب آؤ اور جلد آؤ۔ مجھے کسے
ایک اور ضروری کام بھی جسکا اظہار اس خط میں مناسب نہیں۔

تہاری لڑکپن کی دوست
سونیہ

اصلی ترجمہ تو دوچھ ہوم نساں پر لکھا لیکن شاید اِس چٹھی کو مزار سوں نے تالہ رسوا
میں اِس طرح لکھا ہے۔ اس ترجمے میں اور اَصل میں کمی زیادہ فرق نہیں پڑ۔ ایک
اختلاف البتہ قابل لحاظ ہے وہ یہ کہ سونیہ نے میرے پیارے دوست اکتاب

اب وہ حالت بدل گئی ہو گی
وہ طبیعت بدل گئی ہو گی
خود دینی رہے نہ وہ راقین
اب کہاں میل جول کی یاقین
کہیں ایسا نہ ہو کہ غفلت ہو
شعلے وہ تو اور ذلت ہو
ہم نے مانا کہ وہ بڑی صفات
پھر جائیں مرد ہوں دہ عورت ذات
غرض یہ عورتوں کی طینت میں
اجنبیت ہے ان کی فطرت میں
سب کو دوسرے پر ابری کا سے
آج تک زرم ہمسری کا ہے

یہاں سے ہر وتین شعر قابل غور ہیں۔
اور کچھ راہتے ہوئے اکثر
جب سمجھے گی او نسہ میری نظر
اب نہ جانا ہمارا ضروری ہے
منہ چھپانا ہمارا ضروری ہے
وہ حمایت جو ہے حال پر گئی
نہیں معلوم کس خیال سے بھی
نکتہ الفتہ ای نئی یہ کیوں سمجھو
اس میں یہ پہلو ہے اور یوں سمجھو
بلکہ خوش خلق اور نہیں ہے وہ
صلہ خدمت یہ قدیم ہے وہ
دلہیں جہیم جو ہر پاس عزت ہے
منہ دکھلا نا خلاف غیرت ہے
ذکر اخلاص وہ جہاں لفظہ ای کیا
شکر احسان تقطر زبانی کیا
اس میں ایک یہ غصہ کا پہلو ہے
کہ جہسن طلب کا پہلو ہے
گو کہ احسان جدائی احسان ہے
گر اس میں یہ شرط امکان ہے
نکو اس امکان ہی نہیں پر کیا
کوئی اسمان ہی نہیں پر کیا

مرزا رسوا صاحب کا خیال حسب ظاہر یہ بات چہاں یہ فرماتے ہیں۔
اب وہ کہ پہن کی بات جانے دو
بھول جائو جواب اوس زمانے کو
اوس زمانے میں جو تھی اوسے الفت
وہ محبت ہو باعث نفرت
وہ تیاک اب ہے اوسے پسند نہو
رسم سابق پہ کار بند نہو
بن نے ایخان اگر دیکھا سے
جہیم کرا دل میں کہہ برا مانے
اب یہ فریاد لیا تے اہیں گیر ن
نہیں نجو وہ و ہم جو ہاں میں کیوں
تم بھی نام خدا جو اب اس قابل
تم ہو نہ مہربان کسی کا دل
دوستی اوس سے کبھی نہ بھی کبھی ہوتی
تو بھی اسے دل بتا بچھے کب سے بتی
کیوں عبث ہے حال غیر ہے رسوا
پھر وہی ذکر خیر ہے رسوا

۱۴

اچھا نام نہیں لکھا جیسا جیٹھی یہ موجود ہے۔

مرزا رسوا الٹ اور وہ القا قدآ ورجیٹھی لیکے چلے آئے۔
یہ تائید غیبی صرف ایک مرتبہ نہیں ہوئی بلکہ طالب علمی کے زمانہ میں دفعۃً ہوتی
ہوتی رہی۔ مگر اسطرح کے خطوط سب صاحب کی مرفت آیاکیے اس لیے اکثر
اگون کی بھی حال معلوم تھا۔

اکچھ مدت میں پڑھتے کوئی چو سات برس گذرے ہوں گے کہ مس صاحبہ کا علاقہ
اور جانا دا کورٹ سے چھوٹا ہا ہدوہ کشمیر میں آکر اچھا کو بہی میں رہنے لگیں مگر نہیں
معلوم انہیں کیا ہوگیا تھا کہ مارا تھا نہ کہے۔ اوس زمانہ کے خیالات مرزا رسوا
نے خود نظم کے ہیں اور ہم تقریرپر کیے دیتے ہیں۔ ان مضامین میں جھو شاعرانہ ا آ ورد
معلوم ہوتی ہے مرزا صاحب اپنے خیالات کو ابھی طرح نہیں بیان کرتے بہت
کچھ چھپانے ہیں گم یہ جب نہیں سکنا۔ اس میں ایک خاص بات ہے جس کو
ناظرین سمجھ لیں گے۔

یہ خیال اوسوقت کے ہیں حبیب وہ بہار پریسے آپکی ہیں۔

تغامر سے دل میں ایک وہی خیال	میں ہوں نا دار وہ یار صاحبِ دل
اپنی قوم غیر نہ ہب ہے	بات اتنی بچی جائے جواب ہے

اس میں تک نہیں کہ مرزا رسوا اہمیت بی غیور ہیں اور ا سکے ساتھ ہی طبیعت میں
احتیاط اور خاکسا ہدسے زیادہ ہے۔

کئی بزرگ کئے کچھ خصوصیت	اب نہ وہ لوگ ہیں نہ وہ حالت
کیا عجب سے وہ التفات نہو	پہلے جو بات نہی و بات نہو
گو کہ ہو دل کے جیتے سے محال	کیون کرے جبہ سے محال
غمِ فرقت عذاب ہو کہ نہ ہو	دل مضطرب کو تاب ہو کہ نہ ہو
پہلے سے دل پہ جبر ہی کر نا	اب تاسے جبر صبر ہی کر نا

ہنسے پھر کس دل سے کہا ہوگا۔

مفلسی باعثِ ذلت ہے	دل میں رکھو اگر محبت ہے
وصل کیا یہ خیال ہی کیا ہے	ایک دل ہو وہ مال ہی کیا ہے
چھوڑ دیے اس خیال باطل کو	کرتا دیکھے گا آپ کے دل کو

۳

ومیرافون کی سیر۔ عاشقانہ اخبار پڑھتا۔ یا خود موزوں کرتا۔ مگر ان باتوں سے
دل کی اصلی حالت کا بیان بہت دشوار ہے جیسے گذرتی ہو وہی خوب جانتا ہے
عشق و ہجر کی بلا ہے کہ وصل میں چین نہیں آتا۔ جب کی بیتا ہو ان کو کوئی کیا بیان
کرے۔ بیچ قصیدہ ہے ۔ ع ۔ خدا کسی کو اس آفت میں مبتلا نہ کرے ۔
ہزار سوا کی طبیعت میں دریا کی آگئی کا ان آسی وقت سے شروع ہوگیا ہوگیا تھا مگر اس کے
بعد جو دیکھا ہو تو بجا دے تو گر ما ماری ڈالا۔ مگر ہم اس آخری صدمے کا ذکر بعد میں
کرکے اس کے بعد بعض حالات تحریر کرتے ہیں۔

بھائی کے مرنے کے بعد ان کی کل جائداد ہماری چچا زاد بہن قابض ہوگئیں تھیں۔
چچا نے اپنی زندگی میں جائداد کا ابنی لڑکی کے ساتھ دوسرے جامعہ ام بھائی قابض
ہوئیں۔ تمام کر دین مگر آپ نے نہیں معلوم کس وجہ سے الکار کردیا با جائے خالی با
اس کی وجہ صوفیہ کی محبت جو کہ ان کا حال شیک معلوم نہیں۔ اتنا جانتے ہیں
کہ چچا زاد بھائی بہنوں میں چچا کی زندگی تک پڑ املی رہا مگر جب سے وہ ان کی
شادی ہوگئی وہ محبت ہی الکل عداوت سے بدل گئی۔ اس سبب سے ان کو جائے کے رخ
کے بعد ہی اپنی فکر پڑ گئی غیر خوبی جب ایک زندہ دار ہیں وہ بھی ان کو سیا گیں۔
اوئے مرنے کے بعد ان کو سب سے بڑے کے مشکل پیہ ہوئی کہ رہنے کا ٹھکانا ناہیک
دہا۔ اگرچہ مکان موروثی تھا مگر ننگے والد محبوب تھے اس لیے اٹھا کی ہی عین اسی میں
نہ تھا چچا زاد وبہن کے ساتھ در بنا اور اوٹھ کے ٹھکانے کا نا آئیں میں بھی ہوتا تو یہ
گوارا نہ کرتے اور اب نہ بکار تھا۔ اس زمانے میں ان کی ایک کھلا کی بوا اجیرہ اٹھ کے کام
آئیں۔ اوئیں کے پاس یہ رہنے لگے۔ اسکول میں نام لکھوالیا۔ اگر یہ پڑھنا
شروع کیا۔ اس زمانے میں درحقیقت یہ بہت پریشان تھے۔ تم ایک تائید
شبیہی ہوئی۔ جس کا بیان لطف سے خالی نہیں۔ یہ حال ہکو اک جہم کتب وست
کی زبانی معلوم ہوا۔

اوس زمانے میں انگلس میں ایک ولندیر اپنے در جو میں پیٹھے بڑ رہے تھے۔
استضحی اسکلی کے صاحب نے افضیں بلوالیجا۔ اور ایک لفافہ ایک جیب
سے نکالا۔ اور اگلا اور انگھی چہا کا نام در یافت کرکے کہا کہ تمہارے نام کسی نے
یہ نوٹ سورد ہمہ کا بھیجا ہے۔ تھا خدا در جی ہمارے نام کی ہی۔ مگر کاتب نے

۳

ایک جگہ لکھا آیا ہے:۔

جو اس وقت ہی دل آوری کچھ رہ گئے دل کمان کی ایک ایک ذی جہم جی انبیت بڑھتے ہیں

گر مرزا رسوا نے نہایت استقلال سے کام لیا ہے چنانچہ تحریر فرماتے ہیں

باتیں دن اوسکی کب بناوٹ تھی اوسکی چتون میں کب لگاوٹ تھی

شامت اعمال کی لاگ گئے اوسکی گلیوں کم کر دی بھرے

کیا غرض ہے کہ وہ بلاتے نہیں فرض کیا ہے کہ منہ لگاتے نہیں

تم سے آوارہ کو وہ جا ہے کیوں ایسے دیوانے سے بنا ہے کیوں

تم سے کیوں دل لگائے تم کو کون رنج کیوں اوسکو آئے تم ہو کہ ن

مری نکہیی را ہا احوال ہو گئی غم سے میری دلست حال

غم نے پیدا کیا اتنا دل میں فتور پہلے جو رنج تھے ہوئے ناسور

بیقراری دل لاک کرنے لگی جامہ جیب و چاک کرنے لگی

غم سے حال کبھی کسی سے نہ کہا۔ بلکہ

دل سے اس راز کو چھپا رکھا ضبط کو اپنے آزما رکھا

عشق اور عقل میں لڑائی تھی راہ دونوں زور آزما ئی تھی

میں نے بہت ہی طبیعت کو مرصع ثما لا کیا ایسی آفت کہ

رات دن دل کی لاگ سے جلنا جس سے بہتر تھا آگ سے جلنا

غم محبت آفر رنگ لائی۔ کچھ نہ بن سکا۔

سرے آئی بلا ہمیں ملتی پیچ تو ہے قضا نہیں ملتی

انہوں اسکے بعد کے چند ورق مثنوی نالہ رسوا کے گم ہوگئے۔ مرت واقعات جسلم

ہوتے ہیں وہ تحریر یہ کئے جاتے ہیں۔

قرینہ صاحب ایسا معلوم ہوتا ہے کہ جس صاحب کے مان باپ کے مرنے کے بعد انکی کسی عزیز

نے پہاڑ پر بھیج دیا تھا اور جامہ درد وری کورٹ ہوگئی۔

اس نذر انے نے چند کچھ مرزار رسوا کے دل پہ گذری اور اسکا حال سوا اوگی یا خدا کے کوئی

نہیں جان سکتا۔ مرت نہ یان میں بہی باتیں آسکتی ہیں۔ نالہ وزار کی بیقراری کی حالت

باگا ستارہ گیا۔ دن رات منہ لپیٹے پڑے رہنا لیمک کا جامار ہنا چہرہ کا زرد او ر

بون کا خشک ہوجانا۔ جیلے چیلے دل سے باتیں کرنا بنتشیوں کی صحبت سے نفرت۔

اونکو مجھے کمال الفت تھی   مجھ کو اونسے بہت محبت تھی

پھر بھی قضا نے رحلت کی   اونکی موت نے نہ مہلت دی

آپ کے گھر کا قصہ حال ہوا۔ اور ہر مُنظر۔

اسی انجامین پر گئے صاحب   اس جہان سے گذر گئے صاحب

یہ صاحب بھی گئے بین الین قضا   سو یہ گھر بین ہو گئی تنہا

الغرض دونوں گھر تباہ ہوئے   وہ بھی ہم اور ہر تباہ ہوئے

مگر مرزا رسوا البعض وجود سے ماتم پرسی تک کو نہ جا سکے۔

گو کہ جانا مرا مناسب تھا   لبعض جہوں سے نامناسب تھا

گر چہ دعوے تھا جانفشانی کا   خوت مقام جھکو ہم گس نہ کا

اسلئے کہ سوفیہ کو اپ صاحب کے ایک عزیز نے اپنی خفاظت مین لے لیا تھا وہ مرزا رسوا اور انکے خاندان کے رسم و راہ سے مطلع نہ تھا۔ دوسرے اختلاف قوم و مذہبہ ان خیالات نے روکا۔

گو کہ یاری خبط مجھ کو تھا   مگر ایسا بھی خبط مجھ کو تھا

کہ میری وجہ سے وہ ہو بدنام   ایسی باتوں کا تھا برا الحمام

ایسی ہالت مین مشورہ قربائ دنیائ کے کھانکسے اپنے قلب دل اور اضطراب شوق کورہ کا طبیعت کے استقلال پر دلیل ہے۔

کہ جدائ اسے ضرر پہو چنگے   دور تک عشق کا اثر پہو چنگے

اختلاف قوم و مذہب اور واقعات کی ہیثیت بدلجانے کی وجہ سے خیالات دل مین جاگزین ہو چکے تھے۔

واتفی اوسکو مجھے نسبت کیا   اجنبیت ہو جب تو الفت کیا

کیا کرے سکو وجو کرائ ہو مشتاق   عاشقی بھی سے کوئ استحقاق

اوسکی پایش سے مکرے کو نئ   ایسے مرنے کو کیا کرے کو نئ

مرزا رسوا کا وہ زیادہ شباب کا قصا۔ اب محبت کا رنگ بھی بدل گیا تھا۔

مجھ کو ظاہر ہے خود بھی حال اوسکا   نہ تھا خیال اوسکا

ممکن ہو کہ اوسکی طبیعت مین اس قسم کا فیر جس کا ہسر مرزا رسوا کو ہوا تھا ہنوا ہو۔ وہ اسی طرح لیلی جملے پہلے مٹے ہوتی۔ یہاں کا واہ بدل گئی ہتی۔ اس مو قمر پر مجھ کہ یہ کا

١٠

ذکرِ محبت یہاں واں مین تا ممکن دل دکھاؤں کسی کا کیا ممکن

کس سے یوں چین کد ہرگوشہ دوڑ ہائے افسوس مرگئے وہ لوگ

مزار سوا اور میں صاحبہ آپ میں کھلا کر قصے۔ کیجئے بھی میں محبت دل وان میں لر
کرگئی تھی جیائگا میں واقعہ کو مرزا صاحب نے اس طرح موزوں کیا ہے۔

جبِ زمانہ مین قضا پہ رحم ورا جن و فنِ قتلہ جابیت ان کا نباہ
سرکے سے ہوئی بُجھ الفت بڑھ گئی رفتہ رفتہ کچھ وحشت
بڑھ گیا اور تباہ عہد سے سوا ہو گیا اختلاط عہد سے سرِ ا
دل نازک کا خون ہوئی گیا رفتہ رفتہ جنون ہوتی گیا

مگر یہ محبت یک طرفہ نہ تھی۔ بلکہ کسی اور سے اوٹ محبت کبھی یک طرفہ نہیں ہوتی۔
بسکہ ربط جاننین سے تھا کل اوسے نہی فرین ہی چین سے تھا
سو ان لوگوں پر تفصیرہ نہ تھی بلکو نیک وبد کی نسبت نہ تھی بلکو

ایسی بی محبت تھی جو کبھی ان میں ہوا کرتی ہے۔ مگر یہ بات یہ تھی کہ انہیں ایک مرد
ذات تھا او ودوسری عورت۔ ایسی محبت انجام مین کچھ رنگ سے فرور لاتی ہے۔
مگر اوس زمانہ میں۔

دل میں کچھ خوف والدین تھا میرے دیکھ لینے پین نہ تھا
دوانِ کے دل میں جدا اگر ہوتا کیوں نہ بکو کسی کا ڈر ہوتا
جب ہنو کچھ تو دل میں شک کینا ہو لنے جلنے میں پھر جھک کیوں ہو
واتمی جب بدان میں صفائی ہوتی ہے تو انگریز میں کبھی نہیں چھپتیں۔
سختی صداق بنا پاک الفت تھی مجھے بڑھ کراو سے محبت تھی
وہ لاکین وکیل گودے سن یاد آتی میں ابدومیش کھلاد
وہ زما نہ جو یاد آتا ہے دل چہ رِک سانپ لوٹ جاتا ہے

اس کے بعد اب دونوں ٹلدہ نوچیر خارجی آئی مزار سوا کے جانے انتقال کیا ود اکٹھ بہ دود
کے میچی بہی مرکین بہتر ہے اس واقعہ کو یہ آپ مزار سوا کی زبانی سنئے۔
جبکہ فو نے انتقال کیا میں نے اپنا محبوب حال کیا
یچنے سے اے نبوئگ بلا تھا ہوش جنگ و میں اس بھال تھا

مرزا صاحب کے بہت سی غزلات ہوگا اور نہم تام لکھ دیتے۔

گو کہ وہ سرِ غم خطرین رہے

میم صاحب قیں آؤ دل سو نیک

یہ مصرعہ برا سے بیت پر ہے ۔

دبنیط وارہ پچ وغم سے ودست
طرزدنگار نال م سے درست
شوخی نقش آباد انگیز
اود وہ ولاساقدقیامت خیز

اسکے بعد یو شعر ہے اوس سے معلوم ہوتا ہے کہ رنگت گوری ہی تھی۔ عزنگون کانگ
گورا ہوتا بی ہے۔ مگر اسکا مال تغوریہ سے نہیں معلوم ہوسکتا۔

کیسی سرخ و سفید رنگت ہتی
گور سے جین پراداقیامت ہتی
گرسے پچہ جو آنکھ تک دلبر
اونہیں ہو آنہیں یہ تھک اکثر
اونہین شوخی ذرا نہیں ہوتی
اس بلاکی او انکسین ہو تی

واتھی گورے سے رنگ کے مشوق اکثر یہ تک ہوتے ہین۔ شوخی صباعت کے ساتہ
اور سنہری طلاعت کے ساتہ بہت کم دیکھتے ہین آئی ہے۔
ان مس صاحب کے نسب نسب کے بارے میں عزارسوا فرماتے ہین۔

ایکہے واکا بنافسرانسرملن
اور جاجاتتے ساکن لندن
ہوئے ان باپ ہند مین پیدا
دل سے اس سرزمیج تھے شیدا

مس صاحب خود کہیں مین پیدا ہوین۔ بیدایش کی تاریخ تغوریکی پشت پر تحریر
حقی الوس میں نقل کرنا بھول گئی۔

لکھنو مین یہ خود وہ مین پیدا
تناہی شہر جاے نشو ونما
انکی ولایہ بھی لکھنو کی تھی بت
انکی آیہ بھی لکھنو کی تھی

مادری زبان تو انگریزی تھی۔ گر

یوتی تتین زبان اردو صاف
کس قدر یا محاورہ شگاف
لکنت انگی زبان مین گیا دخل
گفتگ انکے بیان مین گیا دخل

افسوس کہ اردو زبان کا کوئی نمونہ ہمارے پاس موجود نہین۔ جنسے اپنی زندگی مین
کسی دویایت الاصل صاحب بایم صاحب کو با محاورہ اردو بولتے کہ شناو۔ گر مرزا
رسوای شہادت تجا اسے تسلیم کہ نوین۔ مگر کہ چونہ مس صاحب کی ذہانت قابل آفرین ہو۔
انکی تقریر بتی مغد یقامر
بون بچا رنگت قظہ یقامر

عزارسوا اپنے اور مس صاحب کے تعلقات کے دوہ واسطرح تغریر کرتے ہین۔

میرے علوی ناہدار و غیرو
جوکہ ہین سانکشہر مین شہور

لطف تقریر کیا بیان کروں ٭ کیونکر اوسکی ادا بیان کروں

لطف تقریر کے باب میں مرزا نے جو اشعار کہے ہیں واقعی وہ دیکھنے کے قابل ہیں ۔ کیا

نزاکت پیدا کی ہے ۔

جلی قصویر کھینچا ہو محال ٭ کسطرح ہو بیجھے اوسکو رہم خیال

کیا بیان ہو تر اکت تقریر ٭ حیں سے عاجز ہے صنعت تصویر

کاش تصویر بولنے لگتی ٭ رہ تقریر کھولنے لگتی

کیونکر آواز اوسکی سنادوں ٭ خط بھی ہو جار اوسکے دکھلادوں

یہ سب خطوط انگریزی کی زبان میں ہیں مگر صحیح سوچ اور نہیں سے یعنی کا ترجمہ

بہتے کہہ باجے ۔ اوس سے مرزا رسوا صاحب کے قول کی تصدیق ہوتی ہے ۔

طرز ادائے مطلب یا کل بید اسادہ ہے مگر یہ سادگی تکلف سے خالی نہیں ۔

لفظ لفظ مطلب خیز اور نقر و فقر و حیرت انگیز ہے یجے رشک ہوتا ہے کہ کاش

میت ایسی عبارت اردو میں لکھنے لگتی ۔

دیکھ تقریر کی ادا و یژنی ٭ دیکھ فقروں کی آفت انگیزی

گوئی کہ بین یہ کیسی تحریریں ٭ توبے دیکھی ہین ایسی تحریریں

کیا کہوں ہیں تو پر مجلا سوار ٭ توہی کہہ کو لیلظ ہے دیار

نثر عاری میں ایسی ریجینی ٭ سحر ہے سحر کیسی ریجینی

حرف مطلب کا یہی کہیں لکھا ٭ سب لکھا اور کچھ نہیں کہا

یہ طرز تحریر کا بیان تھا ۔ اب اندز تقریر کا حال سنئے ۔ واقعی اسکے بیان میں

مرزا نے کمال شاعری کو صرف کیا ہے ۔

لب و لہجہ میں اوسکے سوبجاز ٭ برق سے بڑھکے شعلہ آواز

اوسپ فقر و کمال موسیقی ٭ دل سے محو خیال موسیقی

کسی اوستاد کی سکھائی ہوئی ٭ دل کافرین لے سائی ہوئی

یہ شعر اور اسکے بعد کے وہ تین اشعروں کا مطلب وہی خوب سمجھ سکتا ہے جسکو

موسیقی میں دستگاہ ہو ۔

اوسکی ہر بات میں تناسبے ٭ چوہرہ است میں تناسبے

کستہ دل حال ڈحال موزدن پر ٭ چال کیسی خیال موزدن ہے

کی حالت ہے اسی طرح کہ آلات نصب بین آدمی کی زبانی معلوم ہوا کہ

۶

کی حالت ہے اسی طرح کہ آلات نصب بین آدمی کی زبانی معلوم ہوا کہ
ایک دیکھنے سے گری سردی، آندھی، مینہ، زلزلے وغیرہ کے حالات معلوم
ہو جاتے ہیں باغ کے ایک طرف جھکو ایک چھتہ بہت گہری باولی دکھائی دی اہم
تو ہے کے سوتوں ہیں سے ایک بہت اونچا برج بنا ہوا ہے اس باولی اور برج
ہیں نیچے سے اوپر تک اندھیرا کنویں ہے دن کو الٹین جلا کے جانا ہوتا ہے
برج کی چھت ہیں جابجا سوراخ ہیں ان سوا آون ہیں سے دن کو ستارے نظر
آتے ہیں۔ اس باولی کے قریب ایک پچھو لائی سی پختہ کوٹھری ہے۔ اسی ہیں گولی
بری وہ رہین کرسے اور کچھ اور سامان رکھا ہوا ہے جسے ہیں ہین کہہ سکتی۔
مرزا رسوا صاحب اور ان صاحب کے حال ہیں جلی یہ کوٹھی اور باغ ہے اس طرح
تحریر فرماتے ہیں۔

ایک ادھ کی تصویر اور تاک کی موزلف   محسن ہیں چہرہ با مستہ بھی سوا
کیا کون بجھے کیسی صورت تھی   سے یہ تصویر ایسی صورت تھی
یہ تصویر خوش فہمی سے ہیں ال گئی ہوتی۔ گم مرزا رسوا صاحب نیچے با مرا رم سے اوپس
لے لی در خدا دسکی نقل ہم مرور ہی شائع کرتے۔

دیکھ نوکس بلا کی صورت ہے   یہی میری قضا کی صورت ہے
یہی قاتل ہے جان بسمل کی   یہی جلاد ہے مرے دل کی
ایسی کا فر نظر نہ دیکھی تھی   ایسی بیداد گر نہ دیکھی تھی
اسی کا فراد اپے مرتا ہوں   دیکھ اس دل ربا پے مرتا ہوں
تو کہ میرا دل تو قاتل ہے   بخدا جانے کے قابل ہے
ہیں کوئی شک نہین۔ ہیں بھی مرزا صاحب کی خوش نظری کی داد دیتی ہوں۔

بخدا چاہنے کے قابل ہے

دیکھ اس چشم نیم باز کو دیکھ   اس نگاہ کرشمہ ساز کو دیکھ
اسین آنکھوں کی جے یہ بیماری کا   اغین زلفوں کی ہر گرفتاری کا
دیکھ ابروین کیا کجھاو ہے   دیکھ نظروں ہیں کیا لگاو ہے
چ کجھاو ٹ کس التیاز کے ساتھ   ہو لگاوٹ مگر ہے ناز کے ساتھ
دیکھ خوبیان تبسم کی   سو پنے بھر خوبیان علم کی

مجھے دیوانہ کیا آپ بنا لو چاہتے ہیں

دشت آبادیں پہ خاص سکونت میری

۳

ہم کہتے ہیں کہ حضرت جب رسوا
بات سے بات کرتے ہیں پیدا
ہے تو عادت نشان اہلِ کمال
اکثر شہرت کی آرزو ہی نہیں
لوگ ایسے بھی ہیں کہیں سلتے
کب کسی سے وہ رنگ ملتے ہیں
ذات پاک ہیں پاک طینت ہیں
اور کی ہر بات میں لطافت ہے
وہ وہابی بھی اور سنی شان کے ساتھ
رعب بھی دابھی وقار بھی ہے
اوتکے اوضاع میں جھلکا نہ
دل میں شرعِ رسول کے پابند
بلکہ ہے سادگی طبیعت میں
گو کہ ظاہر نہو درست ہو
جسم و جان سے تعلق ہے
جی میں اور نکھ سوائے خیر نہیں
عہدِ جاہلیہ کا گیا قرن سے
نورے سے کمال، نادر ہیں
نہ تکلف ہے اور کی عادت میں
ملتے بھی نہیں و شرر فساد
نہ برگشتہ ہیں عیب بین سے کبھی
بے تکلف ان ہم نشین سے بہت
محبت ہو اتنی مہربانی سے
بلکہ اونسے نیاز ہے مجھ کو
اپنی نظروں میں خود عزیز ہوں ان
و رو میں کیا ہر ہی حقیقت کیا

آج ہیں فن شعر میں یکتا
قدردان کیوں ندل سوختہ شیدا
بے نیازی سے شانِ اہلِ کمال
قدردانوں کی جستجو ہی نہیں
ایسے ولیسو کو وہ نہیں سلتے
جرب سے ملتے ہیں جھمکے سلتے ہیں
خوبصورت ہیں نیک سیرت ہیں
اور نکھ ہر شعر میں نزاکت ہے
یہ شرافت بھی ان کے ساتھ
مس موقع کچھ ایک ساری جاں ہے
اوتکے اخلاق میں کر جانا نہ
بہت اپنے اصول کے پابند
ہے کچھ آزادگی طبیعت میں
ان عقیدہ کسی کا سست نہ ہو
دل کو ایمان سے تعلق ہے
صلح کل ہیں کسی سے بیر نہیں
چہرہ ہو اونکو چوہدری قانون سے
دشمن و دوست اہل ظاہر ہیں
نہ قطب ہے اور کی خصلت میں
جانتے بھی نہیں، بغض و عناد
نہ جگر شکن نکتہ چیں سے کبھی
نہیں ثابت جہاں جہیں بہت
یہی بھی ایک اور کی قدردانی ہے
اپنی قسمت پہ ناز ہے مجھ کو
بندگی بھی کہ کر لی چیزے یوں ان
میرا دل کیا ہری طبیعت کیا

منظر آشفتہ پوش سے خالی
سربسر بیدلی و حیرانی

دل بیتاب تاب سے محروم
چشمۂ خون مژگاں بن مژگاں

چہرۂ زرد زعفرانی رنگ
اک پرتوش کا نام و ردربان

دل بیگانہ آشنا ہے کہیں
دین و ایمان نثار کرتے ہیں

پیچ آتی ہے کہ ہے جنوں ان کو
دشمن جاں کو پیار کرنا کیا

جان ہے تو جہان ہے صاحب
دشمنوں کی خراب حالت ہے

عشق سے باز آنے نے آخر
اور پھر ایک بے وفا کے لیے

فائدہ الغرض بیجا سے
آہ و فریاد سے ہوگا کچھ

آرزو سے محال سے حاصل
نالہ نارسا ہے بے تاثیر

یوں ہو بیٹھے بجائے ویراں
قول ناحق پہ جانیے بے عمل

درنہ میں آپ بجے اوصاف
راز دار طلسم راز و نیاز

صاحب امتیاز و ذوق صحیح
تیز طبع دادیب ماہر فن

آپ کا حصہ شیوۂ تحریر
بلا احسان ہے نظم پر قادر

سرشوریدہ وقت پائمالی
موبوحسرت و پریشانی

چشم بے خواب سے محروم
اشک پرشور غیرت طوفان

قطرۂ اشک ارغوانی رنگ
خشک ہو مژگاں پہ آبلہ افشاں

مختصر کہ دل بجا ہے کہیں
کسی کو فکر پیار کرتے ہیں

دوست ہیں سیر کیا کہوں ان کو
اس قدر بے کسی پہ مرنا کیا

اسمیں جی کا زیاں ہے صاحب
عہد سے گزری یہ ہوئی محبت ہے

بس نہیں اب ترک کیجیے یہ طور
آپ کیوں عرتے ہیں خدا کے لیے

فائدہ حسرت و تمنا سے
داد بیداد سے ہوگا کچھ

جس نے وصال سے حاصل
عشق صبر آزما ہے سے تاثیر

آپ سا عاقل اور فرزانہ
ہوا گر کچھ و مانع میں نہ خلل

جل کے گھٹی ہوئیں تعلیم صفات
بدلے نسخ و نظریف و سحر طراز

شاعر نکتہ داں بلیغ و فصیح
کنہ پایا ہے پہ نداق سخن

آپ کا شیوہ و خوبئ تقریر
صفت بزم و رزم پر قادر

یعنی

فسانہ مرزا رسوا

خوبصورت ہو نیک سیرت ہو
اور کیا چاہیے بشر کے لیے

مرزا رسوا صاحب کی وجاہت اور طلاقتِ لسانی میں غضب کی والہ و بیزی جاذبیت ہے جس میں قائل ہیں دیکھ جانے ہیں ۔ عورتیں مرد سب اِن کی طرفت متوجہ ہو جاتے ہیں ۔ جب یہ بائیں کرتے ہیں لوگ بہ تن گوش ہو کر سنا کرتے ہیں ۔ کوئی شخص کیسا ہی غمگیں ہوا انکے پاس دو گھڑی بیٹھے تم غلط ہو جائے ۔ رونے والے آدمی کو ہنسا دینا، ہنسی ایک بات ہے ۔ خدا کی دی ہوئی ذہانت پر ۔ علمیت اور تجربہ کاری ان کی زبان و صفات نے انکے جوہرِ ذاتی کو اور چلا دیدیا ہے ۔ طبیعت کی موزونی تو قدرت نے حسن پرستی کے ذاتی نے چپکا رکھا ہے ۔ ان سب اوصاف کے ساتھ مرزا میں کسبِ قدر بسا ہو بعض طبیعوں کی اثر نا پائی کہ دشمنوں کو جون آوردہ طفل ہے ۔ کسی کو یہ خیال ہے کہ آپ کو پہروان کی سنجیدگی شوخی پر گرفتگ کیجے ۔ کچھ اسرار ضرور ہے ۔
مرزا صاحب کے ایک دل دوست نے ۔ نظم کر لیجے کہ میں نے ۔ آپکے اوصاف مثنوی عالم رسوا کے وزن پر موزون کرتے ہیں وہ بیان حوالہ قلم کیے جاتے ہیں ۔

وحشی آوارہ خانماں ۔ رسوا	ایک مرے یار مہربان رسوا
بیدل و بے قرار بے چارہ	مست و آشفتہ حال و آوارہ
رہروِ شاہراہ ناکامی	ہرزہ گرد و طریق گمنامی
زارو بیمار و بے نور و بے تاب	دل پریشان و منقطع بیتاب
رہنمائے طریق اہل وفا	پیشوائے فریقِ فقر و فنا
بسملِ تیر حسرتِ بیداد	کشتہ تیغ الفت جلاد

۱

ناظرین!

مرزا رسوا صاحب نے جو میری سرگذشت تحریر کی ہے وہ غالباً اپنی نظر میں گذری ہوئی سرگذشت میں اب نہیں کہتی کہ انجھا کیا یا برا۔ مگر پہلے سے اس کا وقار نہ تھا ایسے کسی تقدر لائق ہوا۔ اگر مجھے معلوم ہوتا کہ میری آوارگی کا افسانہ چھاپ کر خلائع کیا جائیگا تو شاید میں ہرگز اس کے جاننے پر راضی نہ ہوتی۔ راضی مرزا اتنا کا مجھ ملہ گیا یہ لطف ہے کہ آپ زمانہ میں میں نے مجھ پر احسان کیا سا کر رفیعت یہ احسان پر تو مین بھی وہ سائر اور سماعوض کرتی ہوں۔

دستنامہ دے کے مجھ کو بہت خوش یہو بیٹے
کیلئے کہ آپ جو میری کا زبان نکلی

مرزا رسوا صاحب کے حالات کا وریافت کرنا سہل نہ تھا۔ یہ شخص میں جو اپنا نام تک لوگوں سے چھپاتے ہیں نہ رہ سے ایسی جگہ میں جہان کسی کی شکل تک رسائی ہو سکتی ہے۔ میں صرف ایک مرتبہ آپ کے دولت خانہ پر حاضر ہو کر اور کسی زیارت سے مشرف ہو بھی ہوں۔ گمارہ و سوقت کہ مجھے معلوم تھا کہ آپ گھر پر نہیں تشریف رکھتے۔ بات یہ ہی کہ جب آپ نے میری سوائح عری کے خالع کرنے کا قصد کیا مجھے بھی یہ ہوگی تھی کہ آپ کے بعض اسرار سدہ ناک و واتف کردن اس کے لئے یم خاص اہتمام کرتا۔ آپ کا ایک ملازم خاص محلے نام و نشان سے میں مطلع نہیں ہے گنتی مجھے ہواف ہو گیا۔

ایک دن آپ ایک دوست کے گھر پر مشاعرہ میں تشریف رکھتے تھے۔ بندی نے فوراً
گاڑی کرایہ کی اور آپ کا کوئی پر پوری کی آپ کا آدمی ہو جب ایک آدمی دسنے چلا جاتا ہے
دکھا دیا۔ اسی آوادی کے ذریعے آپ کی ایک کتاب جس میں ایک تصویر بلوا اور بہت سے
خطوط اور ایک نامہ مثنوی تالہ رسوا سیرہ پاتہ آکی نکھ حالت آبض و سیتی سے
معلوم ہوتے عو کنکہ ان سب دات کو میں نے بطور یہ لگے کے جیب سے لیا جس وقت
مرزا صاحب نے میری سوا جری شالع کی اور اپ جلدا نمی خدمت میں روانہ کی زیانہم
صاحب خوش آہوے ہو نگے۔ شکر کیا رکھے تین ہیں۔

کیم اپریل سن ۱۹۰۹

ندوہ
ادراد جان ادا

ورم از مسوڑھوں و دندان

کبھی دانتوں میں سردی کے سبب درد ورم ہو پراسی کا فوراً ہو جاتا ہے ۔ سردی دانتوں اور مسوڑھوں کی گرم ہوا ریل کیا ، بطلاز حد تاریخ چوں مسوڑھ ہو گیا گوشت جما لنے تنہائتھ کی پیدر کو اور مسوڑھوں کا کفن دور کرتا ہے ۔ دہن کی پیدر کو ران ...